Sabine M. Pereira-Kägi

Embroidered Memories

Sabine M. Pereira-Kägi, born in 1983 in Winterthur, has been passionate about travelling and writing from a young age. After an exchange year in Finland, she returned to her native Switzerland, finished high school at the Kantonsschule Rychenberg in Winterthur, and went on to study Hotel and Tourism Management in Chur. Her first professional role was on a cruise ship, with which she enjoyed sailing the seven seas. After a short stint in the financial industry, where she acquired a Bachelor's degree in Business Administration, she currently works on creative projects in the graphic design field, runs a travel blog and writes. *Embroidered Memories* is her debut novel. Sabine Pereira is married and has a son (*2015) and a daughter (*2016). She divides her time between Winterthur and Flims, a village in the Swiss Alps.

Sabine M. Pereira-Kägi

Embroidered Memories

Klara and Claire, 1939–1945

A Novel

This title is available as e-book and paperback.

The original edition was published in German under the title "Gestickte Erinnerungen" in 2017.

Cover Design: Renzil Pereira

Layout: Ruslan Nabiev

Translation: Sabine M. Pereira-Kägi & Eleanor Updegraff

ISBN 978-3-9524844-3-2

www.sabinepereira.ch

Prologue

After my maternal grandmother passed away and we started clearing her apartment, we discovered a small, non-descript wooden box. Hidden inside it were letters, which my beloved Granny had received in the late 1930s and early 40s, during the Second World War.

At first, the letters – most of them written in French – remained unread. I found it too intimate to browse through such personal belongings. But, after a few years, my curiosity won out. As I read through them, line after line, letter after letter, a story began to unfold – not unknown to me, but the details of which I knew very little of. It was the story of a young woman who fought for the right to live her own life, despite the difficult circumstances and strict social conventions of that era: courageous, adventurous and, to a certain extent, naïve.

It was immediately clear to me that this fascinating story, which is also of great historical interest, should be allowed to have a new lease of life outside the pages of the letters.

With the help of my grandmother's old anecdotes, countless hours in archives and an extensive research trip to France, the letters built the foundation of my story, which is not a biography but a novel – a fictitious reimagining of a true story.

1939

Zug ~ Thursday, 23 March 1939

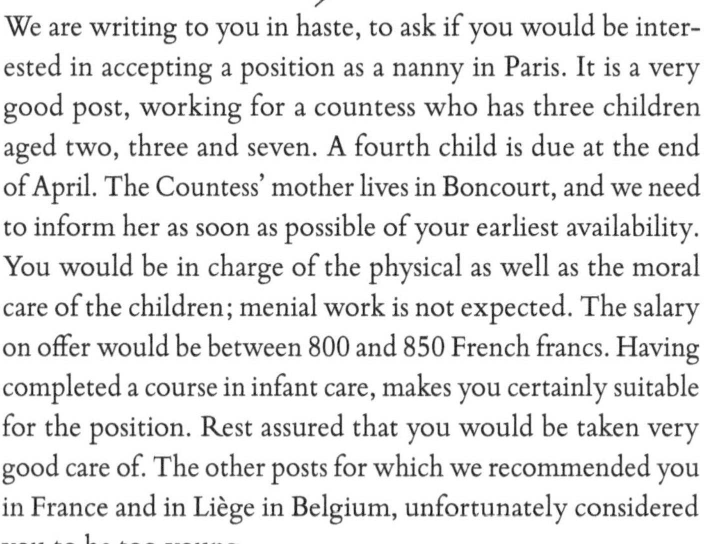

Dear Miss Widmer,

We are writing to you in haste, to ask if you would be interested in accepting a position as a nanny in Paris. It is a very good post, working for a countess who has three children aged two, three and seven. A fourth child is due at the end of April. The Countess' mother lives in Boncourt, and we need to inform her as soon as possible of your earliest availability. You would be in charge of the physical as well as the moral care of the children; menial work is not expected. The salary on offer would be between 800 and 850 French francs. Having completed a course in infant care, makes you certainly suitable for the position. Rest assured that you would be taken very good care of. The other posts for which we recommended you in France and in Liège in Belgium, unfortunately considered you to be too young.

Please let us know immediately – if possible, by telephoning 40272 during office hours, asking for Miss Gyr – if you are willing to accept this offer and the earliest date you could start. We would then recommend you at once.

In expectation of your esteemed, prompt answer, and with sincere regards,

Alice Gyr
Catholic Youth Secretariat of the Girls' Protection Association

P.S. If necessary, please organize a passport as soon as possible.

St. Gallen ~ Friday, 24 March 1939

I have to read the letter several times before I dare to believe it. An offer of a job in Paris — and with a count and countess, no less! It's more than I ever dreamed of. It sounds like a once-in-a-lifetime opportunity and I know for sure that I want to take it. I don't know how much 800 French francs are in Swiss francs, but the salary is irrelevant next to the possibility of living in France. Food and lodging are taken care of; the expenses once I am there will be minimal. The prospect of going to Paris — of actually living there — is more than enough for me at the moment. I am filled with euphoria and have to remind myself not to get too excited — I am not yet holding a contract in my hands.

In the afternoon, I borrow Georg's bicycle and make my way to the public telephone in the post office. In my bag is the precious letter, now covered with my scribbled notes, and some coins for the phone call. I remind myself to keep the conversation as brief as possible; I can't really afford a phone call. Mentally, I go over what I want to say to Miss Gyr: thank her for the letter, accept the job offer with immediate effect and, most importantly, ask her whether she has any idea how I can apply for a passport. Despite the fact that Eugen, my oldest brother who lives in Argentina, must be in possession of such a document, I have no idea how to obtain one. My heart sinks at the thought of the expense involved. But under no circumstances can I miss this opportunity. If I am accepted for the position, I will do everything it takes to make this dream come true. I pedal energetically, as if to shake off my anxiety. I decide to take it one step at a time: for now, I will tackle the phone call.

Sunday, 26 March 1939

Poland rejects Adolf Hitler's demand to return the city of Gdansk against a guarantee of Polish borders, whereupon Germany unilaterally cancels the German-Polish non-aggression pact.

Zug ~ Tuesday, 28 March 1939

Dear Miss Widmer,

With this letter, we would like to inform you that we were notified of your selection for the position with

Madame la Comtesse de Maraberry
10 rue Eugène Labiche, Paris XVI, France

beginning on 1 April. We have been in touch with the Countess' mother, Madame Deschamps, who lives in Boncourt in the Bernese Jura region. Both mother and daughter came to the conclusion that you should travel to Boncourt on 1 April, stay there overnight, and take a train to Paris the next day. Madame Deschamps will certainly take this opportunity to share with you some information that will be useful for the post. We made enquiries in Paris about this very position a few years ago and received nothing but positive feedback. We therefore hope that it is a good match for you and that you will be pleased with your new role.

A new beginning always has its challenges – some greater and some smaller – but with willingness, mutual understanding and patience, it will work out. Should you nevertheless feel disappointed or misunderstood, you should talk to your employers openly and, above all, in friendly terms – that is always the easiest and most successful way of resolving things. Should this not go well – an outcome against which we sincerely hope – you can reach out at any time to the Girls' Protection Association or to the Swiss Women's Home in Paris. If necessary, we are also at your disposal for advice or further information.

You will have a half-day off every fortnight and can perhaps take this chance to visit the Swiss Women's Home. It has been recently renovated and offers the opportunity to meet fellow Swiss ladies. You will also find a library with a wide selection of books.

We are confident that you will not experience any lack of mental or physical wellbeing, and that your stay abroad will be successful and of professional value.

As discussed previously, you will be able to acquire a passport immediately. Your employers in Paris will have to sign your application for a work permit. Kindly let them know the same, to ensure that you receive the permit promptly and do not encounter any subsequent difficulties.

Your photos and certificates are still with Madame Deschamps in Boncourt. Please do not forget to recover them whilst you are there. Regarding the journey, we agreed with Madame

Deschamps that you should travel to Boncourt on 1 April. It will be easy to find the Deschamps family home, Les Chevrières, in Boncourt (telephone 617). If possible, you can inform Madame Deschamps of the train on which you will be arriving in Boncourt.

Unless we hear from you to the contrary upon receipt of this letter, we shall assume that you are in agreement with everything and will travel to Boncourt on 1 April.

The registration fee and placement expenses for your case amount to seven francs.

We wish you a safe journey and all the best for your new position. If you have the chance to occasionally inform us of how you are doing and whether you are satisfied with the position, we would greatly appreciate it. We hope that you remain in good health abroad and send you our best regards,

Alice Gyr
Catholic Youth Secretariat of the Girls' Protection Association

---

Friday, 31 March 1939

Poland's inviolability is guaranteed by Great Britain and France.

St. Gallen ~ Saturday, 1 April 1939

I catch my breath as the train that will bring me closer
to my new life pulls in to the station, hissing wildly. No
sooner have the carriages come creaking to a halt, then bustle
breaks out on the platform. Doors open, people start getting
on and off the train, luggage is loaded from the platform
into the carriages, children are taken by the hand, families
say their goodbyes. I feel like a silent observer of this scene
while, on the inside, my emotions are running riot. Fear,
anticipation, respect for my new assignment and a sense
of guilt towards my family spin around on an emotional
merry-go-round. I pull myself together sharply; after all,
I am in the thick of it now – a traveller. I grasp the handle
of my light brown leather suitcase fiercely, as if it were my
walking stick and gave me a sense of security, and head
towards the train.

Aboard a train to Zurich ~ Saturday, 1 April 1939

The Second Class carriage is emptier than expected, given
the bustle at the station; I have my choice of seats and select
one by the window. Diagonally opposite me sits a middle-aged
man in fine clothing, engrossed in his newspaper. I feel unobserved, which I like. The train pulls out of the station; people
wave at their loved ones with starched white handkerchiefs.
Nobody is waving at me. The farewell at home was rushed.
I had three days between being accepted for the job and depart-
ing, in which I had my hands full. First of all, I had had to tell
my family of the whole undertaking. Up until then, they had
known nothing.

The biggest challenge was having an express passport issued in such a short time. Georg's boss, a respected pharmacist in Rorschach, gave him some useful information about the process of obtaining a passport. This widely travelled gentleman is well informed about such things.

My few belongings were packed swiftly. Thanks to my time in the abbey, packing is routine for me.

The passing trees and soporific swaying of the train remind me of the journey from St. Gallen to Cham, when I used to return after the holidays to the abbey's daughter institute. This time, I will not take the train from Zurich to Zug but travel via Biel to Boncourt, where I should arrive shortly after midday. I hope to find the Deschamps family's house without any problem, as Miss Gyr described it in her letter. I informed the Deschamps that my arrival would be at two o'clock and under no circumstances do I want to be late. The first impression counts and punctuality is a virtue, as Sister Aurora used to drum into us. My biggest worry is my language skills: will my school French be sufficient for me to follow all the instructions and information? Despite my nervousness, I am elated. I am on the road again – what a liberating feeling!

Boncourt ~ Sunday, 2 April 1939

I open my eyes only to close them again immediately, dazzled by the whiteness of the bedclothes. Surprised, I realize that I have slept exceptionally well. I am usually a light sleeper, especially when I have a lot on my mind. It may be that the head of the Deschamps family's confident appearance has made me feel safe.

This slender, dapper man with thick, grey hair and horn-rimmed glasses impressed me with his handshake and calm demeanour when he personally opened the front door to his manor house yesterday. Later, over coffee and cake, he and his wife told me a lot about their daughter's family. Although I had to concentrate, I was able to follow the conversation in French and now know that I will be looking after seven-year-old Paulette, three-year-old Madeleine and two-year-old Aurélie. The fourth child is expected in a few weeks. In the first few weeks after the birth I will be mainly in charge of the three girls; later, I will also care for the infant. Good manners are extremely important to the Count and Countess and they expect me to instil them in their children. But playing, singing and going for walks in the park with them will also be part of my duties. Laundry and cooking will not fall to me, as the family also employs a housekeeper. It sounds like paradise – those tasks were never my favourites and at home I never volunteered to do them. I much preferred to do the grocery shopping.

Yesterday, as I cautiously raised the delicate china cup to my lips, Monsieur Deschamps explained how his daughter left her childhood home in Switzerland after marrying Count de Maraberry and moved to the 16th arrondissement of Paris. I thought I heard a melancholic note in his voice, something I did not expect from a successful patriarch who runs the Parisienne tobacco company with his brother and, as a National Councillor, is heavily involved in domestic politics. But somehow that makes him likeable and human; I took to him immediately.

He explained further that the Count and Countess divide their time between a flat in Rue Eugène Labiche in Paris and

Bon-Hôtel Castle in Ligny, which belongs to the Maraberry family. I intend to look up where Ligny is at the next opportunity. I have never heard of it, but did not dare to ask. Perhaps Ligny is a famous sanatorium or of otherwise importance; I did not want to show any ignorance on the first afternoon.

Carefully, I fold back the duvet and swing my legs out of bed. Against expectations, they do not touch the floor but dangle in the air. The bed in the guest room is a huge, high piece of furniture, decorated with beautiful carvings. I hop to the floor and start my day as usual with light exercises. Stretching, straightening, bending, balancing; just as we used to do in the abbey at half past six every morning before breakfast. At first I disliked gymnastics, but after a while it became routine and I realized how good it felt to start the day actively. My friend Lydia and I always stood next to each other, preferably in one of the back rows.

After my exercises, I wash myself at the basin and get dressed. I fold my nightgown, place it in my suitcase and am ready to leave. Right on top is an envelope, which was given to me by Madame Deschamps the night before. I open it and find, besides my certificates and photos, a smaller envelope. In capital letters, neatly written in ink, it reads 'TRAIN TICKET', but it contains 75 francs. I am touched by the generosity of my employers and determine to send the money to my half-brother Georg at the first opportunity. After all, it was he who paid for my ticket to Paris as well as the passport.

As I walk down the stairs to the parlour I am suddenly nervous. Today is the big day, the day on which I will actually travel to Paris. The pendulum clock in the living room strikes eight. I am on time.

Aboard a train to Paris ~ Sunday, 2 April 1939

The train comes to a halt in the station at Geneva. I am sitting in one of the front carriages. Excitedly, I hold my passport in my hands. The brown cover with the Swiss cross on it is still unscathed. Now, for the very first time, I will cross the border of my country. I am wondering what will happen when two Swiss border guards enter the carriage. They inspect my fellow travellers' documents closely, asking a question or two before moving on to the next passenger. I become aware of the fact that from now on my daily life will be conducted in French. I wonder how long it will take until it becomes second nature, and I no longer realize that a foreign language is being spoken around me. There is not enough time to get nervous before the two men in uniform are standing in front of me. They look stern, compare the photograph in the document with my face and, wordlessly, hand my passport back.

It takes a while before the train starts moving again and continues its journey towards France.

Paris ~ Easter Sunday, 9 April 1939

The first week in Paris has flown by. At the same time, I have experienced so many new things that it feels as though I have been here far longer. Here I am no longer Klara, but Claire. I like the sound of my French name; it sounds incredibly elegant.

Madame is kind but very reserved, and I find it hard to gauge what she thinks of me and my work. I occupy a small room with a washbasin – the first time in my life that I have had a room all to myself – right next to the children's room. In this way, I am able to hear the little ones if they need me, even during the night. So far the nights have been calm, but it remains to be seen what will happen when the new baby is born. It is due any day now.

Today is Easter Sunday. To celebrate this happy day, the resurrection of Jesus Christ, an expansive luncheon was served in the parlour after Mass. To start, there was an Easter pastry filled with pork and boiled eggs, followed by a leg of lamb studded with garlic. I let the unfamiliar meat melt in my mouth, full of enjoyment. Quartered onions and carrot batons gave the clear roasting juices, which were served as a gravy, additional flavour.

I was already full when dessert was brought in. Still, I couldn't resist the 'floating islands', as the Easter dessert is called here. Meringues, carefully poached in milk, floated in vanilla custard. The dish was topped with a cap of caramelized sugar and toasted almonds. The meal was far richer than what I was used to from home, but extremely delicious and carefully arranged. I was impressed. The table was also prettily decorated. Never before have I seen a table on which so much cutlery was laid out for each person. Imposing!

After everybody had cleared his dessert bowl, Madame asked me to wash the children's fingers and mouths and get them ready for a walk. When I returned to the parlour with the little girls, she told me that I would be free until dinner, news that delighted me but also took me by surprise. She and Monsieur wanted to spend the afternoon with their girls.

So now I stand in front of my new home, turn right and head towards the Bois de Boulogne, which, according to Madame, is one of the biggest parks in Paris.

Paris ~
Easter Monday, 10 April 1939

My dearest parents,

A brief postcard from me: the journey to Paris was uneventful and I have already settled in well. My new home is truly princely, I have a room to myself, the children are well-behaved, Madame and Monsieur treat me with great respect. I've been very lucky!

I hope that you are all doing well and send lots of love from afar!

Your Klara – or Claire, as I am called here.

Paris ~ Thursday, 20 April 1939

A new day awakes in Paris and with it the children. Madeleine is already wide awake when I enter the nursery, while Paulette and Aurélie are still dozing peacefully in their beds. I wake the two girls gently as Madeleine washes her face at the basin, unasked. The morning routine is well practised and it doesn't take long before all three of them are washed and dressed in their marine blue school uniforms. I open the window, mild spring air streams into the room, and with the gentle breeze on our faces we head towards the parlour, where breakfast is ready. The girls drink warm milk and eat baguette with jam. I cut the bread into bite-sized pieces for Aurélie; the two big girls eat independently and neatly. Now and again I take a sip of my milky coffee. When the youngest tries to gouge a hole in her slice of baguette with a forefinger, I look at her sternly with big eyes. She flashes a mischievous glance at me but stops immediately and licks her strawberry jam-smeared finger with pleasure.

During the week we don't have much time before we have to set out for school. I check the contents of the girls' satchels, send them to say goodbye to Madame and head off with them. The private Catholic school, which consists of a kindergarten and primary school under one roof, is located just a few hundred metres from Rue Eugène Labiche. Nonetheless, it takes me a good twenty minutes with the three girls; the smallest in particular is always discovering something fascinating and I have to repeatedly urge them to keep walking. I take Aurélie to the kindergarten while the two older girls find their own way to their respective classrooms. I take my time on the way back and enjoy a few quiet minutes.

Paris ~ Sunday, 30 April 1939

The smell of freshly ground coffee dancing with the aroma of fresh baking ensnares me, conjuring a smile to my lips. The deep red raspberries on my *tartelette aux framboises* rise like mountain peaks, sugar-coated like the chains of mountains at home in late summer or early autumn, after the first snowfall. I don't want to think of home right now. Gently, I push the thought away and take a sip of my milky coffee. I was fascinated by the Béchu café from the very first time I saw it; the display with its *brioches, éclairs, pains au chocolat, escargots aux raisins* and long baguettes smells tempting. What I especially like is the attention to detail, the dedication with which the delicacies are arranged. It almost hurts me to see how a saleswoman picks a pastry from the perfect ensemble in order to fulfil a customer's wish. Fortunately, it never takes long until Mademoiselle closes the gaping hole by conjuring up a new piece of patisserie or by shifting the remaining pieces to rebuild the symmetry. I have observed these goings-on from outside several times. It seems that there are always customers here – no wonder, considering all those treats! Next to the shop there is a small café. I have three francs put aside from my first wage: just enough for a coffee and *tartelette*.

I catch myself trying to justify the expense of such a luxurious treat – my parents would think me crazy for doing it. All the bells and whistles – the royal-looking padded chairs, which are more like armchairs with their high backs; the robust yet elegant mahogany tables; the elaborately framed pictures and the curved chandeliers whose lightbulbs resemble dripping candles – would be unnecessary extras for them. I like it.

I listen to the soft strains of Chopin's *études*, which are being played in the background. How many times, without any real success, did I try to master them during my piano lessons in the abbey? In the foreground I can hear the animated conversations of the people sitting next to me. The language sounds melodious, elegant and soft – what a difference to harsh Swiss German! Even though I cannot follow everything, I can understand a surprising amount if I concentrate on one conversation. The French I learned at school was not that bad after all.

Carefully, I cut into the pretty fruit tart. A quick glance at the pendulum clock on the wall tells me that I still have a good hour until Madame expects me back at Rue Eugène Labiche. She asked me to be back for dinner in order to help her with the children. Monsieur is not here this week. If I understood correctly, he is staying in Alsace on business.

St. Gallen ~ Monday, 1 May 1939

Telegram to 0483

Dear sister,
Father passed away last night. Will call tomorrow. Georg.

Paris ~ Monday, 1 May 1939

The words 'Father passed away last night' reverberate in my head. It seems impossible to me that his productive hands should now rest on a white burial gown, cold and pale, in the same way I have seen a few times when attending a vigil for a deceased relative or acquaintance. And how will my mother and siblings cope with the loss?

Numbed by the news, I lie in my bed, incapable of feeling anything. I can't even cry. It seems as if the fact that my father is dead hasn't yet reached my brain. Perhaps it is all just a nightmare. But if it isn't, I have no idea what I will do. When will the funeral be held? Usually they are conducted shortly after the death, three days afterwards at the latest. Should I go home? But I can hardly leave Madame alone in her current state, heavily pregnant and about to give birth any day. The questions turn over and over in my head but no answer comes. The darkness of the night makes everything seem even more desperate.

Madame sits on a stool in the parlour, her stomach huge in front of her. Her favourite armchair, in which she usually reads the newspaper in the morning, must have become uncomfortable or too small. I approach her slowly, unsure of how to start the conversation. But my eyes, red from crying after a sleepless night and the phone call with Georg, give away the fact that something serious has happened. Madame looks at me inquiringly and as soon as I start talking the news bursts out of me. As promised, Georg had called and informed me that Father had died in his sleep on Sunday night. They suspect his heart, but nobody can know for sure. The arrangements for the funeral have already been made. In only two days, on Thursday morning, my father will be buried in the graveyard of St. Gallen Winkeln. Georg was very composed, pointing out in his usual, pragmatic way that it is unrealistic, if not impossible, in terms of time and logistics for me to get home. I should be with them in my thoughts and prayers, and he would keep me posted as to how my mother and siblings are doing. He would take care of everything. My oldest brother, Eugen, could not be reached in Argentina. Willy, a millwright, who has been in Spain on a job for Bühler, is already on his way back to Switzerland. My sisters, Martha and Johanna, are with my mother. Arthur is helping Georg with all the necessary official arrangements.

Madame is as surprised by the news as I am. She formally offers me her condolences and gives me permission to go to church on Thursday morning to pray for my father, having dropped the children off at school. I need only to be back in the afternoon, when the children return. I accept her offer gratefully before leaving the parlour to attend to my duties.

St-Honoré d'Eylau Church, Paris ~
Thursday, 4 May 1939

I kneel on the hard, wooden bench, staring at the bright cross at the end of the chancel as I feed the beads of my rosary, purchased in the Benedictine abbey, through my fingers. I pray an 'Ave Maria', followed by an 'Our Father', but my mind wanders. I try to imagine how the procession with my father's coffin is leaving our house, how he is being carried through the Winkeln district, passing the places he had gone by countless times in his life, all the way to the church. Before mass the church bells will ring, the coffin will be laid next to the altar, the mourners will take their seats and, after a piece is played on the organ, the priest will hold the funeral service. I wonder whether one of my siblings will read a eulogy for our father? Will the people in attendance realize that two of Father's eight children are missing, or will everyone be too preoccupied with their own grief?

The sudden piping of the organ startles me from my thoughts. The organist, who has arranged his sheet music neatly in front of him, must have come to practise – there is no Mass at this time of day. Apart from the musician and me, there is no one in the church. I am not familiar with the melodies of the pieces he is playing, but the sound of the organ never fails to move me anew. A tear rolls down my cheek. I find it incredibly hard to believe that my father no longer exists. My father was a man of few words, but he was my silent hero. What did he think of me as he left this world? I wish I had had the courage to ask him before I embarked on my adventure. He always gave us a lot of freedom. Even we girls were allowed to learn whatever we wanted. There was only one condition: we had to be fully committed. To do anything by halves was unacceptable. Never would I have thought that it would be the last time I would see my father when I left my parents' house on the morning of 1 April. I expect that the reality that he is gone will only fully sink in the next time that I travel back home. Farewell, Papa!

Before leaving the church, I light a candle.

Paris ~ Friday, 5 May 1939

Everything is different this morning. When I get up, the housekeeper tells me with great excitement that Madame was taken to the nearby women's clinic in the night. If not already born, the baby should arrive within the next few hours, she says. As I go to wake up the children I reflect on how I have been touched by both extremes of life – birth and death – within the past few days. My father has begun his journey to the other side and here we are eagerly awaiting the birth of a new child: the circle of life in its entirety.

The girls are excited when I tell them that they will become big sisters today, but they are not in agreement as to whether they would like it to be a girl or a boy. After some back and forth they conclude that their parents would be particularly delighted to have a boy after three girls. And they wouldn't have to share their toys with a brother – he would certainly not be interested in dolls. The latter argument even convinces little Aurélie, who had been vehemently advocating for a girl the whole time.

Paris ~ Wednesday, 10 May 1939

My dear Lydia,

First, I hope that you are doing well. I have been thinking about you a lot recently and hoped for a quiet moment to write to you about all the news from my life – I honestly don't even know where to begin…

You will hardly believe from where these lines are reaching you. Since the beginning of April I have been in Paris, looking after the four children of a count and countess. The youngest, a little boy called Jean, was only born last week. He made big sisters of Paulette, Madeleine and Aurélie, the family's three daughters, and they are filled with pride.

Even now, I sometimes have to pinch myself to make sure that this is not just a dream but my new life! After nearly giving up on my dream of living and working in French-speaking Switzerland, I was offered a job in Paris by the Catholic Youth Secretariat of the Girls' Protection Association. There were only four days between my receiving the first letter and leaving home – four days in which I had to organize the essentials and leave in a rush. The biggest challenge was trying to get an express passport. I had absolutely no idea of how to go about it.

On 1 May I received a telegram from Georg, informing me that our father had passed away. It shook me to the core, especially as I cannot shake off the feeling that I am letting my family down during these hard times. In the daytime I keep myself busy and distracted, but in quiet moments and during the night I am repeatedly overcome by grief.

I hope that I will soon find the time to report on my Parisian life at greater length. For now, I simply wanted to let you know where I am and why you haven't heard from me in such a long time. You will find my current address on the back of this envelope.

I am looking forward to hearing from you and, until then, send my warmest wishes to you in Switzerland!

Yours truly,
Klara

Paris ~ Tuesday, 23 May 1939

With Aurélie in the pram and the two big girls walking beside me, I make my way towards the park. After all those rainy days it feels good to spend some time outdoors. In the warm spring sunshine the flowers try to outshine each other and the girls can hardly wait to reach the playground. We play the 'name game' with the ball we have brought from home – I throw the ball to Paulette and Madeleine by turns, each time saying a name. If it is a girl's name they have to catch the ball, if it is a boy's name they bat it away. If they make a wrong decision, they get a point deducted from the five they started with; the one who is first to zero loses the game. Time and again I am fascinated by how enthralled children can be by the simplest games. I have the feeling that they would continue the entire afternoon. But after three rounds it is time to stop and I send them to play on the swings. I hang my handbag on the pram and sit down on a park bench, the playing children always in sight. I wonder what the summer here in France has in store. Will we be travelling or staying in Paris?

Zug ~ Saturday, 10 June 1939

My dear Klara,

Thank you so much for your letter from Paris! First of all, I would like to offer you my sincere condolences for the loss of your beloved father. What surprising, sad news! I have sent a condolence card to your family in St. Gallen and prayed for your father. May he rest in well-deserved peace!

I hope you are doing well under the circumstances. I was delighted to read that your dream of living and working in a French-speaking area has come true.

I remember wondering about the future on our Sunday walks in Cham as if it were yesterday. To you, it seemed an unattainable goal to live abroad. But even then I could feel how strongly you longed to explore the big, wide world. The Institute at Heiligkreuz Abbey seems to have opened the door to it for you and showed you that there is a lot to be experienced. The sheer thought of returning from our studies to such a sedate town as St. Gallen and getting married there filled you with panic. It convinced me, even during our school years, that you would manage it one day. And now here I am, receiving a letter from my beloved Klara from France!

On my side, there is not so much exciting news to share. I took up my job as a kindergarten teacher in the picturesque town of Zug as planned. I like the work very much; I enjoy the responsibility and invest a lot of time in preparation. I am, after all, doing everything for the very first time. The games, nursery rhymes and songs we learned with Sister Aurora in the teaching kindergarten at the Institute have proven to be a big help and build the foundation of my work.

I get along very well with my colleague, who is in charge of the other kindergarten group. She is very experienced and I benefit a lot from her knowledge. At the moment I am teaching 28 children – a good size to begin with, I find.

My parents and Lotti are in good health, but my sister Louisa concerns us with her delusions. They seem to be getting more and more extreme. She is currently not fit to hold down a job.

My entire family sends you their best regards. They are full of admiration that you had the courage to move to Paris.

On that note and in time-honoured manner I will close for today: a hug and a kiss from Julius, a moustache and a beard from Eduard.

Your Lydia

Paris ~ Tuesday, 13 June 1939

With a smile, I put down the letter. At this moment I miss my dear friend very much. She was always able to believe in me, to listen to me and to make me laugh with expressions like this signing-off. She has a profundity to her character that is paired with lightness and a touch of mischief.

I hope she knows how much I appreciate her words. I get ready for bed in Paris, thinking happily about this valuable friendship, while in Zug Lydia will most likely be asleep already – at the Institute, she liked going to bed early and was usually awake before sunrise. I used to nickname her 'lark'.

St-Lazare Station, Paris ~ Thursday, 13 July 1939

Once again, I stand at the railway station, my brown leather suitcase packed. Next to me, two luggage trolleys are piled high with mountains of suitcases and bags. What Madame has packed for the four days we are going to spend in Normandy is a mystery to me – and, even more so, how we are going to stow it all on the train.

The girls are well-behaved and wait quietly next to me, while the wet nurse rocks little Jean in her arms. Madame looks as elegant as always; you would never guess that she had given birth to her fourth child just a few weeks ago.

When the train comes to a halt in St-Lazare station, it is my job to manoeuvre the girls safely into our reserved compartment. Madame and the wet nurse go ahead; we follow.

The chauffeur stacks the luggage neatly in and in front of the compartment and in just a few minutes we are ready for departure. I cannot imagine what awaits us at our destination. Accordingly, I am very excited; more than the children, who are experienced travellers.

Deauville ~ Friday, 14 July 1939

The setting sun bathes the sea in a special light. On the horizon I spy a ship, but cannot make out whether it is sailing towards or away from the shore.

While we wait to be served in a pretty brasserie facing the seafront, Madame mentions that at today's military parade in Paris, to celebrate Independence Day, British troops marched alongside the French ones. I have a hard time imagining what a military parade looks like. Here in Deauville one would hardly know it was Independence Day; some houses are decorated with the French flag, but who knows whether that isn't always the case.

Madame doesn't comment further on the topic and continues with the fact that she and Monsieur have made plans to spend the summer at Bon-Hôtel Castle, near Orléans. Monsieur wishes to hunt and play tennis; the girls love to play in the forest and fields, and at the nearby lake. For my part, I am already looking forward to living in a real castle.

Our conversation is interrupted. Three waiters place huge platters of fish and seafood on ice in the middle of the table. Each of us receives a small bowl of water, a slice of lemon floating in it. Side dishes such as potatoes and vegetables are served.

The waiters wish us 'bon appétit' and retreat. I am perplexed, having not a clue as to what is lying on my plate or how I am to eat it. I see small creatures, shells, scales, legs and eyes. They seem like having been suddenly overtaken by death.

Once Madame has picked up her cutlery, the girls start to eat. I observe Madeleine, watching how she pinches off the head of a small, pink creature and carefully separates the shell with its many tiny legs. White flesh appears and she eats it with relish. Finally, she nibbles on the tail and sucks out the remains of the edible flesh. I am flabbergasted. It seems to me like a lot of work for very little meat. Madame prompts Madeleine to place the pieces of shell on one of the still unused plates. Afterwards, the little girl dips her fingers into the bowl of water with the lemon slice. At least now I have a vague idea of what each utensil is meant to be used for. It seems as if it is acceptable to eat with the fingers for once. I begin to tackle my plate, taking a bite of the innocuous side dishes to start with before I set about a piece of fish.

Later, walking along the beach to the hotel, I have to giggle to myself about my ignorance. Looking at the children bounding along, I feel lucky that I am getting to experience all of this: seeing the sea with my own eyes and staying in such noble accommodation.

Villerville ~ Saturday, 15 July 1939

After a light lunch overlooking the Atlantic on the sweeping terrace of the Bellevue Hotel, the driver takes us back to Deauville. Madame adores this place, the good air and the noble atmosphere, which are, to her taste, otherwise rather lacking in rough-and-ready Normandy.

Laden with countless bags, we head towards the beach. The wet nurse has stayed at the hotel with Jean. Madame hires two of the colourful beach tents: one for herself, one for the girls and me. The tents are supposed to offer protection from the omnipresent wind and sun. Well-heeled ladies do frequent the beach, but she will under no circumstances become sun-browned like a farmer's wife, so Madame has told me.

The sun is high in the sky and today I am especially glad of the sunglasses which I am now never outdoors without. In Paris they are very *en vogue* and I find it very comfortable to no longer have to squint in the glaring light. The girls are already playing in the sand. Two-year-old Aurélie has been instructed by her older sisters to fill the moulds and buckets they have brought with them with sand. The two big ones build a castle with the sand shapes that are toppled out of the moulds. I wonder whether Bon-Hôtel serves as a model in their imaginations, or whether this is a fantasy construction. I help the littlest girl with her task, dutifully patting the sand down. The girls work very patiently. When they get hot despite the lively sea breeze, we walk the few steps to the sea and bathe our feet and arms. The tide has gone out by this time, exposing its treasures. The girls collect seashells and are fascinated by the crabs that move sideways to shelter in the holes in the sand and disappear, bubbling, into them.

In the late afternoon Madame is in a rush to leave; the tide is coming gradually back in, she says. We learned about tides in our geography lessons, but I can no longer remember how they work and even now, watching this natural spectacle with my own eyes, it is a mystery to me. We leave our temporary, colourfully striped refuge and climb the few steps between beach and promenade. The driver appears as if he was called and packs the bags into the car.

Madame wishes to look around Deauville for a while and so we stroll past the numerous luxury boutiques, which are lined up along the street like pearls on a necklace. She stops in front of a window display filled mainly with wide-brimmed hats adorned with a feather or bow. A young woman in a striped blue top and high-waisted, dark blue trousers opens the door to the boutique with a flourish, greets Madame and invites her in. The door closes behind the two of them and I remain outside, enchanted. This almost boyish lady has captivated me with her energy, confidence and casual elegance. Mademoiselle wears her simple clothes with grace and self-confidence, projecting something magical. Through the window, I watch Madame trying on different types of hat and looking at herself in the mirror. My gaze falls on the big letters above the window display: Gabrielle Chanel. Even her name sounds elegant.

Deauville ~ Sunday, 16 July 1939

Aurélie sitting on my knees, I look out of the train window. With a jolt, the locomotive pulls the carriages out of Deauville station. We are going back to Paris. I can now very well understand why Madame so loves travelling to the Atlantic coast. The constant sea breeze brushes away everyday burdens, relaxing the soul as well as the body. I hope Madame was able to recover from the birth and the first weeks with the newborn. I never know how she is really feeling. Her self-composure both impresses and unsettles me; I feel like a little boat being tossed by the waves while she resembles a solid rock. Any emotion remains concealed to outsiders and I have never once witnessed her losing her composure.

I think of Mademoiselle Chanel. Will she be in her boutique today even though it is Sunday? I would love to be like her: elegant, self-confident, assertive, free.

'Miss?' a child's voice interrupts my daydreaming. 'Are we going to read a book together?'

Paris ~ Sunday, 30 July 1939

The girls have finished their school year. Together with Madame and Inelle, the housekeeper, I have made the necessary arrangements for our stay at the castle. We packed suitcases with huge amounts of clothes and household goods and had them sent to Ligny. Additionally, we had to get the city apartment into shape – a delayed spring cleaning, one could say. I helped Inelle while the girls were at school. Madame had many social commitments and invitations to attend before leaving Paris so I often looked after the children in the evenings as well.

I spend my last free afternoon in Paris in the Bois de Boulogne. How familiar and dear this city has grown to me! It seems as though a new treasure is hidden around every corner; every day I discover something new and yet, at the same time, I feel at home. A pretty café, a façade with gilded plastering, a street lamp of ornate iron, flower-dressed windows, a church with a marble façade, chicly dressed Parisians. It is such a different world to that of home, where the embroidery machine rattles away every day in its dark, dusty room. Who has been operating it since Father's death? Eugen, Jack-of-all-trades, is far away in Argentina and attending to his own business. We very rarely hear from him. I cannot imagine Georg giving up his good position as pharmacist. Arthur runs his own bakery in the Linsebühl quarter, Martha has her grocery store in Rorschach, Willy is abroad most of the time on construction jobs. Then there are Johanna and Julius. Maybe Julius? But he seems to me so young!

Guilt creeps up inside me. I realize that I do not really miss my family and nor do I long for my old life at home.

Paris, Normandy and, from tomorrow, the Loire valley. Now that's a life!

Paris ~ Tuesday, 1 August 1939

Monsieur sits at the wheel of his red Alfa Romeo, Madame with Jean on the passenger seat, Paulette, Madeleine, Aurélie and I in the back seat. Monsieur honks the horn twice, a blithe farewell, as we drive down Rue Eugène Labiche. Everyone is looking forward to the long holidays stretching in front of us. Everyone besides Madame. Or rather, I am not sure when it comes to her. With Monsieur I always know where I stand. Right now, he is looking forward to his hunting trips in the sprawling castle grounds and to tennis matches with his friends. The children are also in best of moods; they can hardly wait to feed the ducks in the castle's swimming lake and to indulge in the fresh croissants that the housekeeper gets from the village bakery every morning of the holidays.

We have left Paris behind us and for a brief moment I think about home. Switzerland is celebrating National Day today, an event for which my family always comes together. All our relatives assemble for the celebrations in our garden, which is decorated with paper lanterns. Everybody brings along something to eat, and we grill sausages over a big, open fire. For the first time in my life, I will be missing this party.

After a rest for lunch, we continue swiftly on our way in the direction of Orléans. Monsieur is keen to reach our destination as quickly as possible. He knows from experience that the children's patience doesn't last forever. I am doing my best to distract them with simple games in order to pass the time. When Paulette and Madeleine have a disagreement about the current score and start to fight, Madame flashes a disapproving glance into the back. I am unsure whether it is meant for me or for her offspring, which makes me feel extremely uncomfortable.

Thankfully, the first castles of the Loire appear shortly afterwards. The girls are distracted. Monsieur tells us that there are over four hundred such magnificent buildings in the Loire valley. The majestic structures with their fairytale gardens rush past us as in a film, and I wish I could stop time to preserve this beauty in my heart. I am scared that I will one day forget what a paradise it is here, or that my memory of it will someday fade. As we come to each new castle I wonder whether it is Bon-Hôtel. I have never seen a picture of 'our' castle. As though she can read my thoughts, Madame speaks up, pointing out an estate that bears some similarity to Bon-Hôtel. This is Montour Castle in Jouy-le-Potier.

Driving past the boundary sign of Ligny-le-Ribault, there is no castle in sight. My legs feel numb from the cramped back seat.

We drive through the small village, passing the village hall, a pub, the butcher's shop, the bakery and the tobacconist. The road curves round behind the church, shortly afterwards we turn left and pass an area of woodland. If I didn't know that Monsieur knew the way, I would be convinced that we are lost. I stare intently out of the window, hoping to finally catch a glimpse of one of Bon-Hôtel's turrets through the treetops. And just like that, our car comes to a halt in front of an iron gate. Monsieur honks the horn, whereupon a middle-aged gentleman rushes up to the gate to open it. As Monsieur steers the Alfa Romeo up the driveway, my gaze wanders over the sprawling, imposing estate and I am left speechless.

Canton Hospital, St. Gallen –
Wednesday, 2 August 1939

Dear Klara,

You probably already know that I have been employed at the Canton Hospital for the past two months. I am very happy with my new position. I work at the secretariat and am always reasonably busy. Since last Tuesday, Margrit von Eggersriet has also been here; she has to undergo an appendix operation and is on the same ward as Emmy Hässig, who had a goitre operated on.

Martha's grocery store in Rorschach is very well frequented, so I often help out on Saturdays. More later on. When are you going on holiday?

Many greetings,
Your sister Johanna

Ligny-le-Ribault ~ Tuesday, 15 August 1939

Carefully, I pick up Jean. I wash his sweet, round face, his neck and his small, knobbly hands and feet, change his nappy and dress him. The little boy chuckles to himself and follows my movements attentively with his saucer-like eyes. Since coming to the castle, the wet nurse is no longer with us and therefore I look after Jean as well as the girls. The baby and

I are already a good team. Together we wake up his older sisters. As usual, it is an easy task to get Madeleine and Aurélie out of bed, especially now in the summer when it is already light outside. Paulette, on the other hand, is hiding under the covers. I manage to convince her to get up after a few minutes. The big ones dress themselves, putting on the outfits I have laid out for them. Afterwards, we make our way towards the kitchen where Antoinette, the castle housekeeper, has already prepared breakfast. The children drink warm milk and eat fresh croissants. I relish dipping my crisp croissant into a cup of milky coffee and look forward to the day ahead.

Ligny-le-Ribault ~ Friday, 18 August 1939

Dressed in a light summer skirt, I sit on a bench in the castle garden. Jean lies in his pram but is unable to sleep. Gently, I push the pram back and forth as the girls play cheerfully on the lawn. Bon-Hôtel lies in front of me in all its white splendour, countless battlements and turrets looming into the deep blue summer sky. I do not know how many rooms the castle has and ask myself whether Madame has set foot in each and every one of them. And all those windows – I have the feeling that some person must be constantly occupied with cleaning them. Once the task is completed, one can start anew.

I beckon the girls over once Jean has fallen asleep. There is still time for a short walk before lunch. We cross the park and leave the fenced property through the back gate. After just a few steps we reach the swimming lake, which belongs to the private castle premises just like the huge woods and a few surrounding farmsteads. I pull a small pouch of hard bread out of my bag, dividing the contents as fairly as possible between the three girls. Aurélie throws her entire chunk of bread to the first duck that swims by and is then inconsolable about the fact that she has no crumbs left for the remaining ducks. Paulette takes pity on her little sister after a while – or else is annoyed by her crying – and breaks off a few pieces from her bread. When all of it is gone, we walk along the path, marvelling at the different flowers and watching a large snail as it crawls across the dry forest floor towards the water, hoping to reach the wet soil before it shrivels. So that we are not late for lunch, I tell the children to turn back and promise that we can return in the afternoon, unless their parents have other activities planned.

Ligny-le-Ribault ~ Sunday, 20 August 1939

Great excitement in the castle. Monsieur has two friends to visit and the men want to go hunting today. Dressed in their hunting outfits, they stand around the big wooden table in the trophy room, its walls decorated with prizes, and inspect their guns. The children are beside themselves with excitement and have asked so many questions that Monsieur called for me. Hunting is a serious affair for the gentlemen. The children are for once allowed to be present during their preparations, but Monsieur asks me to keep them quiet. We watch as they tuck ammunition and provisions into their green rucksacks, sling their rifles and, after a few final discussions, set off. The girls place bets on what the men will shoot today: everything from wild boars through deer to rabbits. Even I am curious to see what the hunters will return home with tonight.

National Exhibition, Zurich ~
Monday, 21 August 1939

To our dear sister Klara,

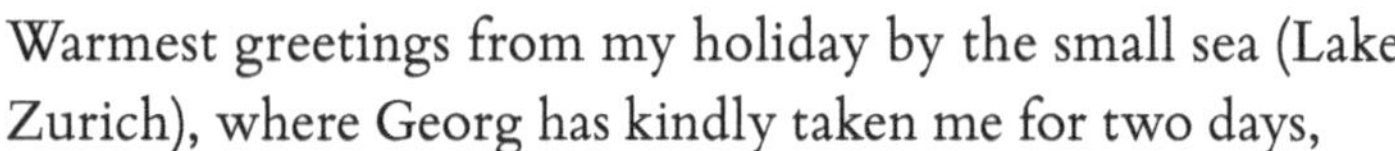

Warmest greetings from my holiday by the small sea (Lake Zurich), where Georg has kindly taken me for two days,

Johanna

What a pity that you are missing out on our beautiful, interesting national exhibition. The cable car across Lake Zurich is a true spectacle; the post and traffic pavillion with the latest technical achievements is informative and interesting. Today there was also a festival of traditional costume. More from me soon.

Warmest wishes,
Georg

Tuesday, 29 August 1939

Switzerland mobilizes its border troops and the next day elects Corps Commander Henri Guisan to General.

Bon-Hôtel Castle,
Ligny-le-Ribault ~
Thursday, 31 August 1939

Despite my tiredness after a convivial evening at the huge
wooden table in the trophy room, where we indulged in a
feast of meat caught by the gentlemen, I pick up a pen and
a postcard of the castle to write a quick message to my family.

Dear all,

A brief sign of life from me so that you know where I currently am. We are in a beautiful castle belonging to Madame
Deschamps, south of Orléans (see the postcard). Surrounding
the castle is a stunning park with a tennis court, just like at the
hotel by the sea!

Newspapers received, also Johanna's letter and the postcard
from Georg and Johanna; reply will follow as soon as possible
by letter.

Thank you very much and best wishes to all of you,
Claire

Friday, 1 September 1939

The German Wehrmacht invades Poland. The Second
World War has broken out.

Bon-Hôtel Castle, Ligny-le-Ribault ~
Friday, 1 September 1939

The silver brooch weighs heavily in my hand – I have a lot of memories associated with it. I clearly remember the day last July when we, the successful graduates of the kindergarten course, received this brooch along with our final reports and diploma. During the graduation ceremony I sat next to Lydia and we listened to the Reverend Mother's speech, sang hymns and afterwards congratulated the newly graduated trade school students and crafts and home economics teachers, who had spent the last two years with us at the Institute.

It was a lovely day. I had dreamed of vocational training for a long time, but it had seemed like an unachievable aim. Thanks to my half-brother Georg's help, my dream came true at that moment. But, at the same time, I was filled with an unexpected emptiness – the interesting days of my education were suddenly over. The uncertainty of the future gnawed at me. I knew with certainty that, with my diploma in my pocket, I did not want to end up in a modest embroiderer's home in St. Gallen, married and with children. I wanted to explore the world.

I had attended French and English classes with the Sisters at the abbey; I enjoyed learning new languages and, in contrast to the artistic subjects, was not completely without talent in this area.

On countless Sunday walks Lydia encouraged me to follow my dreams. 'If you don't take your future into your own hands, nobody else will. Life doesn't owe you anything, you have to take care of it yourself.' I investigated how I could obtain a position in Western Switzerland or in a neighbouring country. I came across the Catholic Girls' Protection Association, where I eventually applied without telling my parents.

I affix the brooch with its image of Heiligkreuz Abbey in Cham, my home for two years, to the collar of my pink silk blouse. Now I am ready for a new day in the service of the Count and Countess.

 Saturday, 2 September 1939

General mobilization of the Swiss Army.

Bon-Hôtel Castle, Ligny-le-Ribault ~
Saturday, 2 September 1939

I look at two serious faces, a lump rising in my throat. Monsieur explains that the President of the Republic has mobilized all available troops with immediate effect. It looks extremely likely that France will go to war against Germany. I sit stiffly on the chair in the parlour and do not know how to react. I have never been interested in politics; I feel foolish for not having paid attention to the latest developments and being completely taken aback by this news. In a matter-of-fact way, the Count elaborates that we will all leave for Paris this evening in order that he may report for active military service tomorrow. We will not yet tell the children, as it would only make them unnecessarily upset. Madame stares vacantly out of the window and bids me to pack my and the children's belongings.

Sunday, 3 September 1939

France and Great Britain declare war on Germany. Both countries have guaranteed Poland's inviolability in the case of a German invasion.

The Western Front remained relatively quiet until spring 1940, apart from small skirmishes and battles. Later on, these months will be referred to as the 'drôle de guerre' or 'Phoney War'.

Paris ~
Monday, 4 September 1939

My dear family,

Only a few days have passed since my postcard from our castle idyll, but a lot has happened in the meantime. We had to leave for Paris in a great rush as Monsieur was called up by the army. He only had one day before having to report for duty. We hardly had time to pack up everything at the castle and return to the capital. The atmosphere is sombre, but otherwise we notice nothing of an immediate threat.

I truly hope that the situation in Switzerland is less tense. May God hold his protective hand over all of us.

I embrace you with all my heart,
Your Claire

Paris ~ Thursday, 14 September 1939

Since Monsieur had to leave for the military and we have been back in Paris, the atmosphere has been very tense. Even though the Countess does not talk about it, I sense that she is extremely worried. War seems to be far away but we are still living in great uncertainty. Madame has heard nothing from her husband since mobilization began. She only knows that his troop is stationed in the Ardennes, close to the Belgian border. I notice that I am also not completely carefree. For the children, everyday life has started again with the new school term. They haven't really noticed that their father does not come home every night – Monsieur regularly used to attend evening social engagements, or was away on business for extended periods of time.

St. Gallen ~
Friday, 15 September 1939

Dear Klara,

Many thanks for your postcards from the castle and from Paris. We all hope that you and your employers are doing well. Have you heard anything from Monsieur since he joined up?

Here in Switzerland the border troops were mobilized at the end of August. Georg, Arthur and Willy have all been called up. Only Eugen, as a Swiss expatriate, and Julius, who is still too young, have been spared. Julius is carrying out all the embroidery work alone, as I am helping in Arthur's bakery. I am trying to keep the business going with the help of one assistant and baker Eggersriet's wife. There is a lot of work but we have to remain calm and circumspect. Take good care of yourself!

With all my love,
Your mother

Paris ~ Tuesday, 10 October 1939

The windows in my room are misted in the morning. As if through a veil I see the street below. The colour of the leaves has changed, yet they still decorate the trees. Anxiously, I get ready for the day. The arrival of autumn sets me thinking. It seems as if winter's harbingers are already hanging threateningly in the air, ready to sweep everything away: the trees are being robbed of their leaves, the streets becoming deserted, the tables and chairs of the brasseries, cafés and restaurants are stored away, even the joy on people's faces seems to be vanishing. It seems to me that in autumn and winter a lot more is cumbersome and mirthless.

Paris ~ Saturday, 21 October 1939

Even on my 21st birthday I do not skip my morning exercises. I start with stretching, then balance on one leg and swing my arms to leave me feeling wide awake. Afterwards I wash myself at the basin, and apply cream to my face, neck, feet and hands before getting dressed. I like the soft, gentle scent of roses that my cream exudes. Roses are always good; I don't know anybody who doesn't like their perfume. Before I go to wake up the children I apply some powder to my face and coat my eyelashes with black mascara.

As I sit at the breakfast table with the girls, Madame appears in the doorway and wishes me a happy birthday. She encourages her daughters to do the same. Three small pairs of arms wrap themselves around my neck, which is not quite as etiquette commands but touches me deeply. In this moment I realize how much I have grown to love these children. Madame asks me to stop by the parlour after breakfast before we leave for school, which we accordingly do. With few words she hands me an opulent bouquet of autumn flowers and a small present prettily wrapped in pink paper with a decorative, cream coloured bow. I am moved all over again and, seeing my emotion, Madame smiles a rare smile. The girls clamour for me to open the gift right away. When Madame nods in agreement, I start to undo the beautiful bow and open the paper. A leather case engraved with my initials, C. W., appears, in which is a pair of beautiful brown sunglasses. I can hardly take my eyes from this magnificent object, but Madame urges us to leave. As we go, she tells me to take a few hours off. I only need to pick up the children when school is over, but until then I am free. I thank her warmly and set off with the girls, leaving Inelle looking after Jean.

How different a scene to that of past years, I think, strolling through the Trocadero gardens with my handbag and new

sunglasses. The dry leaves crunch under my feet and I am happy and grateful for Madame's generosity, for the care with which she picked a suitable gift for me and for the love I am given by the children. The doubt that sometimes overcomes me as to whether Madame is truly happy with my work seems swept away in an instant. I pass the Warsaw Fountain and the Eiffel Tower comes into view.

Paris ~ Friday, 27 October 1939

The first snow of the season fell today and it is only 27 October! The children were extremely excited and pressed their little noses flat against the window, watching in fascination as the snowflakes danced from the sky, floating thickly to the ground. Madame was annoyed about the marks left by the children's noses on the panes. She seems to be very tense. I wonder whether it has anything to do with the latest political developments. She hardly talks about it, especially in front of the children, and I find it difficult to get to grips with current world events. Very rarely do I get a glimpse of a newspaper or otherwise access the news.

Paris ~ Friday, 17 November 1939

'**N**anny,' I hear a well-known voice whisper. 'I'm scared, I'm scared of dying.' Half asleep, I swing my legs out of bed, step into my slippers and throw on my dressing gown. I take Madeleine's hand, her bare feet slapping against the cold stone floor as we head towards the children's bedroom.

As on the previous nights, I sit on the hard edge of her bed and hold her small, warm, child's hand tightly. My head keeps sinking forward; I am close to dozing off. I catch myself yearning for the instant where the pressure of her hand will slacken as the little girl drops once more into a deep sleep, so that I can go back to bed myself. It is exhausting. I am used to a lot of work but not to this much lack of sleep. The days seem to be never-ending and I long for evening so that I can sleep. During the day my eyes keep getting heavy and my patience is not at its best. It is astonishing what effects chronic lack of sleep has on one's body. I ask myself how my parents managed to raise eight children without much external assistance. Only now do I realize what a mammoth undertaking that was. In spite of myself, I ask myself whether I ever want such a definitive change in my life. I love children, but right now I cannot imagine giving up my freedom.

Paris ~ Sunday, 3 December 1939

What an emotional roller coaster! Until recently, my mood
was fogged by a coat of melancholy. Heavy as a velvet cape,
it pressed down on my shoulders and I found it difficult
to convince myself to even go outside. Now I am happy that
I managed to pull myself together to come out today; a hot
chocolate with whipped cream in my favourite café is a true
wonder weapon! Within an instant my sadness evaporates. I let
my thoughts wander and don't even notice how the artfully
arranged whipped cream is slowly losing its shape and melting
down the side of the cup. When I finally catch sight of the
cup I have to rush to prevent the whole treat from landing
in the saucer. Slowly and contentedly I eat the cream, mixing
the rest into the hot chocolate.

A young couple is sitting next to me, little older than me.
They seem to be discussing their plans for the future, their
forthcoming nuptials in the spring. He could imagine spending a few days in Brittany, while she dreams of the South.
Italy or Spain – if one is already in Biarritz, Spain is not really
far away, she argues. A honeymoon should be something
special, something one doesn't do again any time soon, she
continues. He, on the other hand, is of the opinion that
the wedding celebration will already be making a big enough
hole in their pocket and that a few days in Brittany would
suffice. Especially in these uncertain times, he maintains,
it is advisable to have a nest egg. I admire how the young
woman has her own opinion and speaks it aloud. What will
that mean for the future of the couple? Is he aware of the
fact that his fiancée has a strong character and her own point

of view? Perhaps he admires her and found her attractive for it in the first place.

I start to envision what qualities I would wish for in a life partner. It's not that easy, I realize. I would not be averse to a charming, classy Frenchman from the South. But would such a man remain faithful or seek to practise his charms on other Mesdemoiselles? Probably not a good choice.

Perhaps an intellectual, well-read writer whom one would meet in a bistro in the Marais quarter, reading the newspaper with an espresso in one hand. Or possibly a glass of white wine, come late afternoon. With this kind of man one could enjoy life to its fullest, philosophizing and debating. In summer one would drive to the ocean; the salty breeze, the fish dishes, the wine and pastis on the terrace in the evenings would almost certainly be inspiring enough to get rid of any writer's block in an instant. But whether an author's work is lucrative or this choice would spell out a penniless future, I don't know.

I decide that I still have time to establish what kind of characteristics my future husband should have. At the moment, I can't imagine entering into such a binding relationship. As well as responsibility it means a lot of compromises, or so it seems to me, thinking about the conversation I have just overheard. I drink the rest of my now-lukewarm hot chocolate, pay and set off for home. Dusk has already started to fall.

Paris ~ Monday, 11 December 1939

Given that Monsieur is still at the Front, I have recently taken to accompanying Madame and the children to social engagements. Yesterday, after church, we had accepted an invitation to lunch with Madame Mirabaud, an old friend of the family – an occasion which continued into the early evening. Yesterday should actually have been my free afternoon, so Madame has given me a few free hours today instead.

I march through the cold streets of Paris in the hopes of making some purchases for the upcoming holidays. I would like to send Christmas presents to my family and Lydia in Switzerland and to buy small gifts for Madame and the children. I hope that the postal service to Switzerland is working. Madame told me that she is expecting post from her parents, but according to her father it is repeatedly 'returned to sender'.

Sunk in my thoughts, as I pass, I watch a few children skating on a frozen pond in the Bois de Boulogne. The icy temperatures of autumn and winter have frozen many bodies of water. The children seem to enjoy it, while the adults struggle with the high prices of coal and try to keep their houses warm without using up all their coal supplies before the year's end – this at least I learned yesterday from conversations at Madame Mirabaud's house.

I reach the stationer's on Avenue Victor Hugo. The bell above the door announces my arrival and I am greeted warmly. The selection is large and I happily choose two festive cards printed with French Christmas greetings. They seem very special to me and I imagine how the card will be given the place of honour in our kitchen in St. Gallen. I also consider what I could get to please Madame. It is difficult to find a present for somebody who has everything and is able to fulfil all her material wishes. I choose a small guardian angel made of paper, which is prettily packed in a small box and could be hung next to the ornaments and baubles on the Christmas tree. I will whisper lots of good wishes for Madame to the angel – above all, that this war, which doesn't yet seem to have properly broken out here but is still causing so much uncertainty, will soon be over and that peace will return. Before I go to the till, I ask for a couple of nicely packed coloured pens; I would like to give them to Madeleine as she loves to draw.

I continue on to the toyshop on the same street. There I find a pretty doll with a china face for Paulette. I will surprise the wild, energetic, animal-loving Aurélie with a wooden puzzle picturing a farm. Little Jean will get a colourful wooden rattle. I am pleased with my purchases and look forward to giving them to their recipients, even if I don't yet know how we will be spending the holidays. Madame keeps quiet in this regard.

Paris ~ Friday, 15 December 1939

I like the spirit of Advent and try to spread it here as well. Madame, who grew up in Switzerland, has organized an advent wreath with four Bordeaux-red pillar candles, a tradition that isn't usual in France. Last week I baked *Mailänderli* with the children. The smell reminded me of home, where we baked all sorts of cookies every year. My favourites are

the cinnamon stars, but they are time-consuming to make –
one leaves them to dry rather than baking them – and didn't
seem suitable. At home, we always sang festive carols while
cutting out Christmas cookies in the kitchen, and so today
I also sang with the children after school. By now I know
several French children's songs but no Christmas carols, so
I quickly taught them the German song 'Oh Christmas Tree',
which they are now belting out loudly in a sweet accent.
At least Paulette can sing the words; the younger two find
them difficult to understand. In hindsight, I am not certain
whether in these times it was a good idea to come up with
a German song and teach it to the children.

Zug ~
Wednesday, 20 December 1939

Dear Klara,

Thank you very much for your Christmas card, which I was
delighted to receive. I am glad to hear that you and your
employers are well.

In these uncertain times, I wish you with all my heart a cheerful and reflective Christmas. I pray for more peaceful times
in the coming year. May wisdom and foresight guide all those
charged with important decisions.

Enjoy your first Christmas abroad! I wait in great anticipation
to hear your report on the celebrations across the border.
Which traditions are common in France? Do any of them
remind you of our customs or is it all completely new to you?

I am well but am very worried about Lotti, who has been living in the South of England since her marriage. Luisa also causes us concern. As her condition didn't improve, she had to be sent to the insane asylum on Lake Zug, which is very difficult for us all to come to terms with. Genius and insanity are really very close to one another.

On this note, blessings from your friend,
Lydia

Paris ~ Sunday, 24 December 1939

The finely made figures in the crib disappear in a cloud of incense. The priest takes his duty very seriously and circles the crib once more, swinging the incense holder. I am slightly dizzy from the perfumed vapour and am pleased when we – Madame, the children and I – are able to go out into the fresh air. The children are dressed dapperly and look enchanting in their sweet woollen coats, red hats and scarves. After we have wished our acquaintances a 'Happy Christmas', we set off for home through the darkness. During mass, I noticed how few men were in attendance. Those present were either still boys or the aged. The other men must be serving in the army. I wonder whether these countless soldiers will be celebrating Christmas, far away from their families. Will they at least be given something special to eat in the barracks?

As far as I can tell, nothing is lacking in Paris – at least not in Madame's house. The table is generously laid when we enter the warm apartment. For the *Réveillon*, as the Christmas feast is called here, we eat goose with chestnuts, liver and cabbage.

Afterwards, the traditional Bundt cake and small sweets are served. It is nearly midnight and the children are so tired that their eyes are almost closing, but these treats must not be missed. Full of excitement, they go to bed voluntarily after the meal so that Father Christmas can leave their presents under the decorated tree during the night. Before I go to bed I look for a suitable place under the tree for my presents. I give Madame, who is also occupied with wrapping presents for her children, the little paper guardian angel. This time it is she who is moved. Unusually for her, she hugs me, and I sense that her heart is heavy.

1940

Paris ~ Wednesday, 10 January 1940

Jean lies thickly swaddled in his pram as I push him through the biting Parisian cold. It is my first winter in the French capital and I am astonished by the consistently low temperatures. There is not much snow, but I can barely remember the last time that the mercury climbed above freezing.

With my precious cargo, I steer in the direction of the Bois de Boulogne, as I often do for a short walk when the girls are at school. In the park I meet several mothers who, like me, are walking with children, and older people taking their dogs for a walk. The inhabitants of the capital always seem elegant to me, even when they have just popped out with their children or pet. Elegance seems to be an unwritten rule here. This winter the women wear knee-length, fitted wool coats, often camel-coloured. The waist is additionally emphasized by a belt. Gloves in the same colour as the shoes give every outfit a certain amount of style. Even in the depths of winter these ladies don't cut any corners when it comes to their outward appearance; for walking in the park, most of them wear pumps or heeled winter shoes that lengthen their legs.

I love these hours in the park with Jean, which give me the opportunity to study the fashions of Paris and him the chance to take a nap.

As I leave the park through the Porte de la Muette, I muse on what the new, still-young year has in store. I wish that everything would stay the same, at least as far as my little world is concerned. Of course I also wish for world peace,

but am overcome by the quiet foreboding that this is too big
a thing to ask. The threat of war unsettles me. I have heard
that food is going to be rationed. I don't know how that will
happen and what it will mean for my everyday life, so I prefer
to banish such oppressive thoughts from my mind.

Monday, 22 January 1940

The Swiss army begins to march north – units are
regrouped and the Alps more heavily defended.

Paris ~ Monday, 26 February 1940

Happy third birthday, little Aurélie! In the morning, before
I took the girls to school, I gave her a little present that she
opened without hesitation and in high spirits. Her sweet
laughter, a carefree giggle, goes straight to my heart. A deep
bond has developed between me and the children over the last
eleven months. The kind of love that I feel for them is something I've never experienced before.

Now I am looking forward to the afternoon with the girls
and hope that Jean will have a long noon nap as usual. Then
Aurélie will be allowed to choose some games, before friends
and relatives come to visit in the evening. One must be well-behaved in company and so the little bundle of energy will have
to rein herself in. I sometimes think that occasions like this are
not really child-friendly, and serve rather for the enjoyment

of the adults. The children will be expected to keep 'as still as a picture'. But no matter, I am not one to judge.

Gare de l'Est, Paris ~ Wednesday, 20 March 1940

My suitcase is packed and I am waiting for the train at the Gare de l'Est. What awaits me at home? I haven't been there for nearly a year, have missed birthdays, Christmas, Easter and the burial of my father. Interestingly, I didn't get struck by homesickness even during the holidays – I enjoyed spending these special occasions somewhere else for once. Who knows how often I will have such an opportunity during my life! I am certain that it is more difficult for my family as my usual place at home is empty – or so their messages leave me to understand. By comparison, they have no set place in my Parisian life. Of course I often think of them and am looking forward to seeing them again in a few hours, although I am slightly worried about how I will feel about my father's absence.

My gaze falls on the piece of paper in my hand:

Ministry of Tourism, Paris, 20 March 1940

Holiday approval

The employer, Madame de Maraberry, herewith confirms that Miss Claire Widmer, Swiss citizen, is employed by her as a nanny and will return to Switzerland for a holiday for five weeks, from 20 March 1940 until 27 April 1940.

The document is signed by the French Ministry of Travel and Madame, and will allow me to exit and re-enter the country. I am grateful to Madame for allowing me to return home for five whole weeks. Five long weeks. It's crazy – what on earth will I do with the time? 'Adieu, Paris, and *à bientôt*,' I ponder, as the train rattles out of the station.

St. Gallen ~ Thursday, 21 March 1940

There is a quiet creaking and cracking when I tread on the frozen grass. I have an unpleasant feeling as I approach the row of gravestones. Father is in the third row from the front – since his death, countless graves have been added. I remember Sister Ruth's saying that death is always happening. An elegant wooden cross marks the grave. My mother has already picked out a massive gravestone of Tessin granite. On the first anniversary of his death, it will replace the wooden cross.

I slowly unwrap the protective paper from the flowers that I bought from Mrs Egger and hope that the delicate blooms won't be frozen in a few hours. The splash of colour looks good in the otherwise bleak landscape of the cemetery. For the first time in a while I pray 'Our Father' and 'Ave Maria' in German. Subdued, I step from one foot to the other. I am cold. Nevertheless, I want to visit my stepmother's grave. The mother of my half-siblings Eugen, Georg, Arthur and Martha died giving birth to her youngest child and left my father a widower with four young children. Is it a strange thought for my mother that her husband is now reunited with his first wife in Heaven?

What a to-do! I am happy if I can retreat for a short while to my old, childhood room. Everything looks just as it did before – unchanged and static, as though time has stood still. We have just come back from Easter Mass and Winkeln also looks as it always did. The same church, the same priest, the same Mass, the same people, the same discussions. I was happy to see neighbours, acquaintances and relatives again, all of them hanging with great curiosity on my every word, hoping to catch a piece of abroad from my lips. But the interest didn't last long before village gossip began to dominate again.

Strange, I think. Somehow I had expected that something would have changed here too. So much has happened in my life – how can everything here be the same?

The Easter meal is about to take place and many relatives have made their way to our front room. Such feasts usually happen in our house as we have space and my mother likes to play the hostess. I open the door of my room, go down the steep wooden stairs and look forward especially to the sweet Easter cake – one made with semolina and raisins, not with rice.

Ligny-le-Ribault ~
Thursday, 4 April 1940

Dear Miss Claire,

I hope that you found your family in the best of health. Your loved ones must have been very happy to see you again.

I heard of your misfortune, but learned from Mrs Deschamps that you were at home for Easter. We miss you very much and are waiting with great impatience for your return. Since you left, Jean has stopped eating – he loses weight every day. The girls talk about you all the time. Madeleine is really very sad that her nanny is no longer here.

I have had a lot to do since your departure, but fortunately Inelle came from Paris to help me. Antoinette is not available at the moment as her husband has gone to the Front and her mother is bedridden, so she has to look after her children.

You must get in touch with Mrs Deschamps regarding your return; she will take care of your visa. Stay at home until the 24th and then leave the next day, so that you will be with us on the 25th.

Enjoy your holidays! Best wishes and see you soon,
Countess de Maraberry

St. Gallen ~ Monday, 8 April 1940

Smiling, I put the letter aside. The grapevine between
Boncourt and Paris seems to work perfectly; otherwise
Madame wouldn't know that I had waited on the wrong
platform and so missed my connection in Geneva during my
journey home. Fortunately, another train had been travelling
to East Switzerland just two hours later so I had reached home
with only a slight delay.

St. Gallen ~ Wednesday, 10 April 1940

Grey-blue fog is creeping through the town park even in the
early afternoon. The bare trees reach up to the darkening
sky like bizarre skeletons. There is a mystical, almost divine
atmosphere: threatening and, at the same time, as soft as a
cotton-wool ball.

I am on my way to the Old Town. The scarcity of cars
on the streets is noticeable. Catching sight of the tower of the
Monastery Church, which I can glimpse from here, my heart
grows warm. This must be the feeling of being home, I think –
a feeling that is strange to me. In our religion lessons the slightly
senile priest Pfaff told us countless times that this magnificent,
sacred building of the late Baroque period has nine bells and
three organs: the big Cathedral Organ in the West Gallery
as well as the Epistle and Evangelic Organs in the Choir.

We girls always giggled, which the priest – who was not only
senile but hard of hearing – never noticed. As long as I live,
I will never forget the facts that he repeatedly drummed into us.

Zug ~ Sunday, 14 April 1940

When I get out of the train carriage at Zug station, my dear
friend is already waiting for me. Lydia hugs me happily. 'Wow,
Klara, don't you look elegant with your handbag, gloves and
sunglasses! You've turned into a Frenchwoman in just a few
months! *Très chic.*'

She whistles through her teeth. Laughing, I answer that
I feel very at home as 'Claire'. We link arms and stroll to our
favourite café in the centre of Zug. I immediately feel safe and
happy, as though we hadn't just met each other for the first
time in over a year. Once we have each ordered a piece of traditional cherry cake and a pot of coffee, Lydia tells me about
her job as a kindergarten teacher and her new flat, which she
recently moved into with Mauzi, her cat. Lydia has always
loved cats. When we used to go for a walk each evening after
our studies, she couldn't pass a cat without stopping to stroke
it. I, on the other hand, never much liked these furry animals.
I find them unpredictable. Mauzi was allowed to move with
Lydia from the family home to Zug. I admire her for her
decisiveness, for how she goes her own way. While I tend
to question everything and often overthink the details, she
always knows which way to go. She also has a few pieces
of news from the abbey, as she occasionally returns to nearby
Heiligkreuz for Mass and chats with the nuns and students.

I report in detail on my new daily routine, life in France
and my trips to Normandy and the Loire Valley. I sense Lydia's
genuine interest and tell her how enlivened I am by discovering
new things, even if it's only trying different kinds of pastries

or visiting a new café on my day off. Even grocery shopping, which I always enjoy doing, is a little adventure every time.

The hours fly by and when it's time for me to take the train back to St. Gallen, I realize how much I miss having a trusted person, to whom I can speak about everything, in Paris. We embrace for a long time, not knowing when we will see each other again.

St. Gallen ~ Wednesday, 24 April 1940

At the beginning of my holiday I wondered what I would do at home for five long weeks. Now, on the day of my departure, I realize that my holiday at home has truly flown by and I was never bored for a minute. I spent a lot of time with my family, talked to my mother for hours and noticed what a remarkable woman she is. After my father's death, which caused her a lot of pain, she took her life into her own hands and is now looking confidently towards the future. She is grateful for her children and enjoys her work in the embroidery shop, even though the golden years of this tradition-rich handicraft seem to be over. Nonetheless, she carries out her embroidery work with pride, especially when she is given complicated patterns intended for export. She is also running Arthur's bakery since he was called up by the army.

Besides this, I enjoyed Nature, went for lots of walks and experienced my St. Gallen through the eyes of a traveller. I noticed lots that I hadn't seen before and looked closer at things – the many beautiful paintings on the old buildings, for example. Sitting in the mild spring sun on the wooden bench in front of my parents' house, I devoured books that I had wanted to read for ages but had never got round to. I feel rejuvenated and am looking forward to my return to Paris.

Paris ~ Friday, 26 April 1940

While I was enjoying my holiday and amusing myself at home, bad luck struck several times in France. During my stop in Boncourt, Madame Deschamps told me that Monsieur had been badly wounded in the leg during a skirmish at the Front and is now in a military hospital. Everyone is very worried about whether the leg can be rescued or will have to be amputated. Just a few days after Madame had received these evil tidings, Paulette broke her leg playing at school. After her initial treatment in the local hospital, Madame decided to send the eight-year-old to recover in Normandy; she wouldn't have been able to care for her well enough herself, having to look after little Jean, Madeleine and Aurélie as well.

I feel awful and can't get rid of the feeling that I abandoned Madame during this difficult time. Madame Deschamps tried to calm me and assured me that the Countess had expressly forbidden her to tell me the news during my holiday.

Normandy ~
Saturday, 4 May 1940

My dearest Nanny,

I hope that you had a nice holiday. My cast was taken off on 27 April. I am walking very well again. I miss you a lot.

Is Madeleine eating well? And how is my little sister Aurélie?
Please tell Mummy that I cry a lot over her and Jean.

I embrace you with all my heart, Mummy too!
Paulette

Friday, 10 May 1940

The beginning of the Western Offensive. Germany
attacks the Netherlands, Belgium, Luxembourg and, in
doing so, circumvents the Maginot Line: a system of
defensive bunkers along France's borders with Belgium,
Luxembourg, Germany and Italy.

Paris ~ Saturday, 11 May 1940

My dearest Mother,

Thank you very much for your card. I assume that by now
you have long been in possession of my news. We are staying
in Paris for the time being: Madame, Madeleine, Aurélie, Jean
and I. Paulette returned to us yesterday from her recuperation
in Normandy.

Aside from that, the little ones are doing very well. Monsieur,
on the other hand, is having difficulties. He had to be operated on again and it's still not clear what will happen with
his injury.

And what hasn't happened politically! Last night, at around five, Paris was woken by the howling of sirens. The air raid warning lasted until around half past six – terrible. Lots of activity in the air. Countless people are leaving Paris again; we are staying. In the holidays we will go to Deauville on the coast. How are things in Switzerland? Hopefully the ingenious person will not dare to trouble us as well.

Tender wishes,
Your Claire

Tuesday, 14 May 1940

Swiss civilians flee urban centres to the Alps.

Paris ~ Wednesday, 15 May 1940

Deafening! The shrill sound of alarm bells breaks through the curtain of sleep – not a bad dream, but reality. I startle awake, pick up the two smallest children, wake the older ones – who, amazingly, are still asleep – and go with them to the air raid shelter. The process is already routine; half asleep, I go down the gloomy stairs, Jean and Aurélie balanced in my arms. Fortunately, Paulette is able to walk so well by now that she makes it down the stairs alone, albeit limping and with help from the porter. Madame has also come; like a ghost, she flutters towards the protection of the cellar in her silk dressing gown. It doesn't take long before the sound of the sirens mixes with the drone of fighter jets.

We can't do anything but hold out, and this inability is awful. At least our refuge is under our apartment building. When the alarm sounds, many Parisian citizens have to hurry to safety in a metro station.

To my astonishment, the two smallest children have fallen asleep again. I try to keep them in the land of dreams by rocking and humming to them. Paulette clings anxiously to her mother and worry is even visible on the Countess' face. I wish I could also sleep through it all. What is all this in aid of? My heart bleeds for my beloved Paris. War has caught up with me.

Paris ~ Monday, 3 June 1940

Please, dear God, may this be over soon! For the first time in my life I am afraid of death – real fear that forces its way into my innermost being. We have sat together in the cellar countless times, huddled against one another, crouching on the floor and holding out in silence. But this time everything is different. The dull explosion was nearby, shaking us to the core. It felt as though the different parts of my body didn't know in which direction to move, as if it was about to burst. The children whimper, which seems worse to me than violent crying when they have hurt themselves on something. They too have realized the threat here.

I wonder where the bomb landed. Is our building still there? Does it feel like this when one is buried? Did it hit the neighbouring building? Or Mrs Paillard's flower shop at the end of the street?

I look up and into Madame's face to see a single tear rolling down her cheek.

Paris ~ Tuesday, 4 June 1940

Our chauffeur, Bruno, returns with full cans of gasoline. The decision is final: we too will leave Paris. Just like so many others in the last few days and weeks. Bruno has been trying to get hold of the rare and valuable fuel for days; I have no idea where he finally managed to find it. Or at what price.

We pack the waiting suitcases and bags hastily into the car. As much as possible is to be brought to the castle, as according to Madame the German army is approaching the gates of Paris and nobody knows what will happen if the capital is occupied. The plan is for us all to drive to Ligny. If there is enough petrol and it's still light, Bruno will come back for another load of possessions to carry south, like the silver tableware, the valuable cutlery and a few furs. Time is of the utmost importance, as curfew comes into force at dusk. But even a suicide squad wouldn't risk going out onto the streets after dark, given what has fallen from the sky in the previous nights.

Fully laden, we drive off. After the car was packed, Bruno had tied a few boxes tightly to the roof. Melancholically, I remember our last journey to Bon-Hôtel Castle, last summer. Back then we were all full of joy and looked forward to the holidays with excitement. Now this is a farewell for an unknown length of time, into an uncertain future. Madame has sat in the front next to Bruno with Jean, Inelle has Madeleine on her lap, Aurélie is on mine and Paulette sits between us, so that she can stretch her injured leg out a little bit in front of her. It is very quiet – no one says a word, but follows his or her own train of thought. Several of the churches and official buildings that we pass are stacked half to the roof with protective sandbags.

We drive past an endless stream of refugees. People walk or ride bicycles, horses, donkeys and carts. Everyone carries as much as they possibly can; prams, wheelbarrows and even empty birdcages are laden with objects. Even the smallest children who have just learned to walk carry big packs. Fear, exhaustion and uncertainty are written large on every face. The crowd of people in front of us makes it nearly impossible to pass. We move forward barely faster than if we were on foot.

I watch as a heavily pregnant woman kneels by the side of the road, doubled over in pain. Will she give birth here? Further along the road, a huge hole gapes beside the carriage-way. The earth smells burned. 'Shell hole,' murmurs Bruno, and I have the dull sensation that the burned pieces in it used to be people. The body of a horse is also lying next to the road. I don't want to look any more. In the midst of the misery I am aware that we are privileged, even if we don't know what awaits us.

Tuesday, 4 June & Saturday, 8 June 1940

Aerial battles between the Swiss and German air forces over Ajoie. Three Swiss and eleven German planes are shot down.

Ligny-le-Ribault ~ Monday, 10 June 1940

War – the very word and the fact that I am supposedly
in the middle of one – seems surreal and too much for me.
Up until a few days ago I knew of war only from my father's
and grandparents' tales: stories of scarce food, fear, uncertainty and absent fathers, brothers and other male friends
and relatives.

My daily life at the castle is quieter and more straightfor-
ward than in the previous weeks in Paris. The girls don't go
to school here and so Madame has asked me to teach them
in the mornings until she has found a suitable governess.
Every evening I consider how I can teach the girls reading,
writing and mathematics. I don't have much experience
in this. At the moment it doesn't look like we'll be able
to return to Paris any time soon, and finding a governess
seems to be difficult in the current situation. The children
don't really understand what the word 'war' means, but that
doesn't mean that they don't sense the fear and oppression.
By now they have found out what has happened to their
father. Sensitive Paulette asks especially often about him
and can't understand why her Papa can't simply come to the
castle to heal his injured leg, as she did in Normandy. We
can do nothing but hold on in the hope that this terrible
war won't last too long.

Ligny-le-Ribault ~
Tuesday, 11 June 1940

My dear family,

I wanted to let you know that we too have had to leave Paris.
We are currently at Bon-Hôtel Castle. The days before we
escaped and the journey to the castle were nerve-wracking,
but now we are in safety and hope that it will stay that way.

I am only aware of a little of what is going on outside France.
I can thus only hope that you are all doing well. I am thinking
of you!

With love,
Your Claire

Friday, 14 June 1940

The German army occupies Paris with no resistance.

Ligny-le-Ribault ~ Saturday, 15 June 1940

While Madame, Inelle and I try with all our might to make daily life for the children carefree and regular, the German army is – as Madame predicted – parading on the Champs-Elysées. The city's best hotels have been occupied and, apparently, turned into command centres. It is said that the Commander in Chief of the German army is quartered in the Majestic Hotel on Avenue Kléber, and that a red swastika flag flutters on the Eiffel Tower.

I don't know from where the Countess gets the latest news, but it worries me. Other news of the war also affected me, but now it is all so near – so reachable and threatening.

I am now happy that I have the girls' education to throw myself into. It distracts me. While I have Paulette read aloud, the two small ones can be copying letters. They do this with a lot of enthusiasm and patience, at least for a certain amount of time. Afterwards I take over and we look at a book about ducks together. I try to explain to them what the birds eat, how they build their nests and how baby ducks are hatched from an egg. Later in the afternoon we will have the opportunity to watch ducks living in the wild on the nearby pond. The extensive castle grounds are an idyllic scene that can hardly be beaten!

🔍 Monday, 17 June 1940

German tanks reach the Swiss-French border at
Pontarlier.

🔍 Saturday, 22 June 1940

A truce between Germany and France is signed in
Compiègne Forest. France is divided into an occupied
and unoccupied zone, the latter called Vichy France.
The two areas are separated by a demarcation line.

Ligny-le-Ribault ~ Sunday, 23 June 1940

'Who won: you or us?' a young officer snaps at Bruno. I flinch
but, as Madame has ordered, try not to show that I understand
everything. She thinks that it could be dangerous if the Germans
notice that I can follow all their conversations. Bruno, who hasn't
understood a word of what was said but must have realized by the
tone that he has been snubbed, retreats uncertainly. I also try
to make myself as invisible as possible.

The German officers appeared out of the blue like a swarm
of crickets and have billeted themselves in the castle. We are toler-
ated, but have had to move into the small rooms on the top floor.
One of the first things to happen was that all the clocks in the
house were put forward by one hour. We are now on German
Reich time.

Inelle has to cook for the officers, who make sure that they have a good time: meat, which we only ate sparingly, is set on the men's table every day. They smoke, drink good wine from Monsieur's well-kept wine cellar, play cards and pose for photos in the castle gardens. It almost looks as if they are on holiday here.

The safety in which we had felt ourselves to be was a misconception.

Ligny-le-Ribault ~ Tuesday, 25 June 1940

I watch from my window as a large table and countless chairs are carried into the castle park. Inelle brings the family's monogrammed white tablecloths. An enormous amount of crockery, silverware and the best crystal glasses follow. The kitchen maid wears white gloves to polish the cutlery before setting the table. Then she carefully holds each glass up to the sun, removing fingerprints and fine particles of dust with a cloth. After a short while, a celebratory table has been prepared.

High boots gleam in the sun as Lieutenant von Winterfelt enters the castle garden. He takes the seat at the head of the table and tells his officers to sit as well. Champagne is served; von Winterfelt makes a toast and then stands up abruptly. The officers follow suit, the glasses are raised and 'Heil Hitler, Sieg Heil!' echoes through the idyll of the summerlike garden.

I lower myself into a chair and pick up a book. The sound of voices reaches me from outside and I can smell the sweet perfume of the linden blossom.

A bang startles me from my reading. I rush to the window, peer cautiously out into the gathering dusk and am witness to a breath-taking firework over the lake. As the last sparks fall into the lake like glow worms, torches are lit around the table and music begins to play. Contentment is in the air as the officers exuberantly celebrate the truce. I don't remain hidden. One of the officers calls up to me cheekily, 'Mademoiselle, may we offer you a glass of Champagne? Please come and keep us company.' I am annoyed by my own curiosity and retreat to my bed in the hope that I will soon be forgotten.

Ligny-le-Ribault ~ Friday, 28 June 1940

I return to the castle with two bulging shopping bags. What I saw in the little village confused me. It is full of an unusual, happy bustle and teems with foreign uniforms. Soldiers saunter through the streets or sit in groups in cafés and bistros, having a good time. Placards written in German are fixed to walls, reading 'Those who plunder will be shot.'

As I walk up the drive, a good-looking officer hurries towards me.

'Mademoiselle, may I help you with the bags?'

Before I can reply, the charming boy – who can't be older than twenty – takes the load from me and carries the shopping into the kitchen. I follow his white-blond mop of hair. His profile reminds me of Julius. Who is waiting for him at home? A mother, a sister, perhaps even a wife and children? The well-built, able-bodied man turns and looks at me with his ice blue eyes. I can't imagine him in battle. Are those soft hands capable of killing? My gaze falls on his black Mauser pistol and wanders from there to his leather belt with a buckle engraved with the words 'God with us'. Without meaning to, I thank him; he nods and turns to go. His boots thunder on the floor. He has the unmistakeable walk of a victor, a walk that scares others and doesn't suit his young face. As I leave the kitchen, Madame suddenly appears in the doorway.

'That is our enemy, Claire.'

Ligny-le-Ribault ~ Sunday, 30 June 1940

Madame doesn't want to stay. She doesn't trust the occupiers, although they have treated us respectfully so far and allowed us to stay in the castle. She thinks that after France's capitulation we are no longer safe in the occupied part of the country. Our escape plan has been made. Under the pretence of going to Sunday Mass, as usual, we will drive to the nearby village and be picked up by a trusted friend. I don't know any more than this. What is certain is that we can't take anything with us but our usual handbags and the Sunday clothes that we will be wearing. Bruno, the good soul, has already smuggled a bag of things for the children into the car. We have no idea what would happen if the Germans found out about our escape plan. Would they let us go, prevent us from leaving or even worse?

We leave the castle, perhaps for the last time, and drive through the forest in the direction of Ligny. Madame and I are visibly agitated, but Bruno gives nothing away. Inelle has stayed behind – it was her express wish – which fills me with great fear, unease and also incomprehension. Behind the church, feeling unobserved, Madame greets her confidant and we get into a bigger car. We leave Monsieur's car behind. With our backs to the church, we drive along the only big street in the village, passing its characteristic red brick houses with their white, green or red shutters. I try to soak up everything I can of this idyll, not knowing if I will ever return. I like travelling, but being on the run is something entirely different. The constant uncertainty and upheaval are hard to cope with.

Madame tells her daughters that if we come to a police or military checkpoint they are not to say anything but must sit in stony silence. I infer from the conversation between Madame and Monsieur Bouchet that we will be travelling south, to Biarritz. I have no idea where that is but it must be quite far away – we cannot cover the remaining distance in one day. We will have to spend one night on the road and stop in Bordeaux in the late afternoon.

Bordeaux ~ Monday, 1 July 1940

Dear Inelle,

I forgot my passport and identity card and would be incredibly grateful if you would send them to me by poste restante to Biarritz as soon as possible. They are under the books on the second shelf in the cupboard behind the curtain in the second-floor children's room.

In gratitude,
Claire Widmer

Demobilization of the Swiss army to around two thirds
of its previous size.

Biarritz ~ Monday, 8 July 1940

I feel miserable; my tears don't want to stop. I lie tired and
worn-out in bed, wanting only to sleep but unable to escape
the torturous thoughts of my missing documents. The ten-
sion and exertions of the past weeks have left traces – on the
children as well. I can hardly conceal my frustration over my
scattiness. Madame doesn't blame me at all. She is, on the
contrary, very helpful – together, we provided the Swiss
Consulate with the necessary information to get me a replacement identity document. I just feel indescribably awful for
having to add to her burden with my problems.

Biarritz ~ Wednesday, 10 July 1940

CERTIFICATE

The mayor of Biarritz confirms herewith that Miss Klara
Widmer, born 21 October 1918 in St. Gallen, Switzerland,
evacuated from Paris, employee of Countess de Maraberry,
attended the mayor's office in Biarritz on 10 July 1940 for
the purpose of identification.

Swiss Consulate, Bordeaux ~
Friday, 12 July 1940

Dear Miss Widmer,

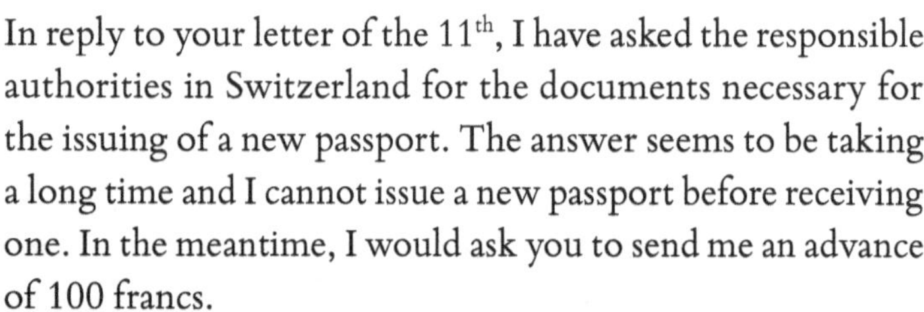

In reply to your letter of the 11th, I have asked the responsible authorities in Switzerland for the documents necessary for the issuing of a new passport. The answer seems to be taking a long time and I cannot issue a new passport before receiving one. In the meantime, I would ask you to send me an advance of 100 francs.

In addition, please have the enclosed *Signalement Fiche* (registration form) filled out by the mayor and counter-signed, and return it with two photographs.

Respectfully yours,
The Swiss Consul
On behalf of the Vice Consul

Biarritz ~ Monday, 15 July 1940

100 francs is a tidy sum. Still, I am happy that the Swiss authorities continue to be efficient and reliable even in times of war, so I will gladly pay the required amount – around the same as a whole month's pay – myself.

The réduit strategy of the Swiss army: the most important part of their defence measures, which are based on the principle of dissuasion. A combination of a staggered defence (split between border troops, mobile troops moved forward into the centre of the country, and strongly fortified centres in the Alps), the planned destruction of important North-South links and the probability of a long, loss-heavy campaign in difficult-to-access mountain regions, should have a deterring effect on the enemy.

Swiss Consulate, Bordeaux ~
Friday, 19 July 1940

Dear Miss Widmer,

Further to my letter from the 12th, I can inform you that I have now received the confirmation of citizenship from St. Gallen and am thus able to issue your new passport upon receipt of the documents listed in my letter from the 12th.

In expectation of these and sincerely yours,

The Swiss Consul

Biarritz ~ Wednesday, 24 July 1940

Warm, tingling waves of happiness and relief wash over my body as my gaze comes to rest on the gentle surging of the Atlantic. I can hardly believe my luck; I would never even have allowed myself to dream that I might one day see the sea with my own eyes again. But now I am standing here, my lemon yellow summer dress tickling my legs as it flutters in the salty breeze, as though it wants to shake me and say, 'Wake up, this isn't a dream!' The glittering surface of the water has something magical about it; the glimmer reminds me of the crystals on my grandparents' Christmas tree.

The waves break slowly and measuredly on the beach. How do they come into being, out there in the wideness of the sea? The deep blue stretches as far as my eyes can see; it seems to never end and yet one knows that somewhere, hundreds or even thousands of kilometres away, there is land. What could be happening over there? What do the people look like? Are they also, like me, strolling deep in thought along a promenade? What do they dream of and is there war over there too? Although war seems so far away from here right now – unlike in Paris, where the wailing of sirens and the awful thundering of bombs accompanied our nights. During the day it was quieter, but one's breath quickened at the thought of darkness falling again in just a few hours. The news was equally oppressive. But Biarritz seems to have been spared everything thus far – it seems like paradise.

Contentedly, I sit down on the little stone wall that separates the promenade and street from the beach, my handbag next to me. I shudder at the thought that this awful war still enables me to experience such wonderful moments of happiness. Without the increasing threat in the capital and, later, at the castle, we probably wouldn't have fled and I would never have had the treat of this view. I wonder whether that is a bad thought and if in such times I should be allowed to feel so happy and lucky that it borders on euphoric.

No satisfying answer comes to me straight away and so I try to get rid of the stubborn, oppressive thought by concentrating on a group of happily playing children. They play catch in the sand, carefree and with an enviable lightness of being. What a blessing!

St. Gallen ~
Thursday, 25 July 1940

Dear Klara,

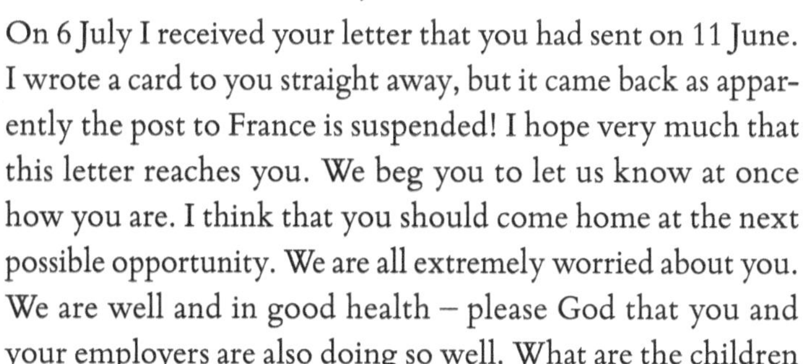

On 6 July I received your letter that you had sent on 11 June. I wrote a card to you straight away, but it came back as apparently the post to France is suspended! I hope very much that this letter reaches you. We beg you to let us know at once how you are. I think that you should come home at the next possible opportunity. We are all extremely worried about you. We are well and in good health – please God that you and your employers are also doing so well. What are the children doing and how is the Count?

Please let us know as soon as possible or come home!

Biarritz ~ Tuesday, 30 July 1940

There seems to have been no space left on the card for
a signature, but I can definitely tell that this is my mother's
handwriting. Just a couple of days ago Georg sent me a telegram with the same request. I am not happy that my family
are despondent and worried about me. My mother especially
seems sick with anxiety about me since the loss of my father;
I have the impression that my letters and cards asserting that
I am well don't calm her in the slightest. I decide to send
a message home at the next possible opportunity.

Biarritz ~ Saturday, 10 August 1940

In front of me is the Biarritz lighthouse, standing imposingly
on the cliffs in defiance of the weather. Every morning and
evening I take a couple of minutes to look out at the sea from
my bedroom window.

By now a daily routine has established itself here in the
South. The girls are tutored every morning by a governess,
during which time I mainly take care of Jean, like today. We
are to do some shopping in the nearby St-Charles district. I set
off on foot along the tree-lined street that will take us from
Villa Kerlys to the town centre, Jean sitting in his pram and
observing the world around him with alert eyes. In just a few
minutes we reach the pretty St-Charles district, where one
small shop follows another. The streets are lively and the dis-
plays in the shop windows abundant, unlike recently in Paris.
The prices, however, are astronomical – I wouldn't be able
to afford most of what is on my shopping list. The prices seem

to be no problem for Madame, whereas the occasional lack of items is. Varied and sophisticated dining is important in her household – she doesn't shy away from any of the efforts that are necessary in these difficult circumstances to serve a constantly changing menu. Although she doesn't cook it herself, she decides personally on the menu and plans the shopping.

With my long list, I head in the direction of the fruit and vegetable shop – my first stop. The owner, whistling happily, greets me with two fingers held to his hat. He packs my requested items in paper bags with much care and composure. I pay what he asks and head for the butcher's.

I can hardly get enough of the immense variety; I love the different smells and colours and the freshness of the goods on offer. What a pleasure! The French have a talent for celebrating beauty, even in these hard times.

My last stop for today is the Cherrier bakery on the corner of Rue Albert. I buy baguettes and *friandises* with the household money that was given to me. Madame is expecting friends for coffee in the afternoon. To his delight, Jean gets a biscuit, which he devours with relish on the way home. One can already see the little boy's *savoir-vivre*, I think, and have to smile.

Villa Kerlys, Biarritz ~
Sunday, 18 August 1940

My dear family,

Yet again two months have passed since you last heard from me.
And so much has happened in these past weeks. I hope that this
letter finds you all in good health and that these difficult times
are not weighing on you too heavily. I am well – you really
don't need to worry about me. You will, however, be astonished
to learn that I am not writing to you from the castle or from
Paris, but from even further away. We had to leave Bon-Hôtel
in a rush after it was occupied by German officers. The whole
situation was very nerve-wracking and increased by a frustrating
mistake of mine: in the agitation of our escape, I left my documents in the castle and had to be issued a new passport by the
Swiss Embassy in Bordeaux, which fortunately worked out.

Madame, the children, Bruno (the butler from Paris) and
I escaped with a confidant from Ligny to Biarritz. Biarritz
– as you are surely wondering – is on the Atlantic coast near
the border with Spain. Perhaps you can look up in the atlas
where I am living now. The situation is quiet here and we
are safe. I like it very much; we are living in a big villa near
to the sea. When I have the window open at night I can hear
the waves and see the sweeping light of the lighthouse.

There is one more piece of news: Monsieur is with us again.
The second operation in the military hospital managed to save
his leg and he was released a short while ago. His left leg, however, is lame and walking is very difficult for him. It is hard

to watch how a once agile man has to drag himself forward with difficulty. We all still hope that he will recover fully.

As you can see, there is no reason for you to worry about me. Georg's telegram and Mother's card were both forwarded to me here.

On that note, I close with sunny wishes from the Atlantic coast!

Your Claire

Lourdes ~ Friday, 23 August 1940

The seats are comfortable, at least for a pew, I think, clasping my rosary as I admire the Virgin Mary statue at the end of the grotto. Today we have come to Lourdes, at the foot of the Pyrenees, in order that Monsieur may bathe in the spring in the Massabielle Grotto. In the 19th century, the Virgin Mary appeared here several times to Bernadette, a poor, young girl, after which the spring in the grotto was said to have healing powers. Apparently miraculous healings happen regularly, or so Madame told me, and she too hopes that Monsieur's crippled leg will be miraculously healed by bathing here. I imagine that the visit is accompanied by a generous donation in the hope that this might also contribute to a healing.

Madame and the children accompany Monsieur to his bath in the spring water, while I wait up here in the grotto to pray for Monsieur's healing, as requested by Madame.

I notice with annoyance that my thoughts are slipping away from prayer. I can't concentrate and, instead of piously chanting 'Our Father', watch the people around me: the very ill, who perhaps only have a short time left to live, paraplegics, spastics with cramped necks and contorted faces, the mentally disturbed. Having made a pilgrimage here, they pray, light candles and sometimes speak to fellow sufferers, confident in their belief that their illnesses, injuries or discomforts of old age will be healed.

A young woman sits down next to me. She must be around my age. She folds her hands, sinks to her knees and begins to pray reverently. It looks like she has urgent pleas for God. I turn my gaze to the Madonna and once again try to pray. Halfway through my 'Ave Maria', I suddenly hear words of Swiss German, clearly understandable though they are murmured quietly. Amazed, I turn to my left, from where the words seem to be coming, and hear myself ask, 'Do you speak Swiss German?'

The young woman, who had been sunk in prayer, turns round sharply. She doesn't seem to be angry with me, although I addressed her informally without knowing her, and looks at me incredulously, yet laughing.

'Yes,' she says, and hugs me spontaneously. I feel an unusual connection to this stranger, even though we have never seen one another before. The fact that we are both Swiss seems to create an immediate sense of familiarity in our foreign surroundings. As though we had discussed it, we both get up and walk in silence to the grotto entrance, where we sit down on a stone bench. Only here do I notice the band on her left arm with the symbol of the Swiss Red Cross.

'My name is Käthi,' says the young woman. 'Who are you?'

I introduce myself as Claire and ask what brought her from the safety of Switzerland to the South of France. She taps her armband, which she wears over a grey, knee-length coat, and explains that she is a Red Cross nurse stationed not far from here, in Gurs internment camp near the city of Pau. Up until recently, most of the inmates were Spanish Republicans – political asylum seekers or former fighters – who had fled the Franco regime. But now more and more gypsies and Jews are being brought to the village of barracks fenced in by barbed wire. I learn in what terrible circumstances and with what primitive means the volunteers try to reduce the inmates' suffering. Käthi and her colleagues defy the pitiable conditions in the hospital barracks. Bugs of all sorts, such as bedbugs and lice, and people's terrible fates are their constant companions. The hardest to bear are the empty gazes of children's big, hungry eyes, which seem even larger in their wan, shrunken, aged faces. They try to wash every child and baby at least once a week. What they see then moves Käthi to tears even as she tells it: children's bottoms suppurating with abscesses, backs full of open sores, bellies bloated with hunger, infected stumps of amputated limbs, stinking wounds.

The conditions are not fit for humans and can only be marginally improved by the relief supplies brought by train from Switzerland. Everything is lacking: hygiene supplies, bandages, nappies, clothes, food and blankets.

Käthi's descriptions get under my skin, boring into my insides like painful pinpricks. While I am enjoying a life that is comfortable despite the war, she deals voluntarily with this immeasurable suffering, hoping that she can have a positive effect on even a handful of people's situations. I admire her bravery and moral courage and ask her how she can withstand this human misery.

She looks at me with her clear, alert eyes and says, 'Shortly after my arrival, I made friends with an interned young woman called Jaël. One day, the French camp administrator came to our barrack with a list on which were countless names. We had to round up these people, a train arrived and they were told to get on. They were standing there pressed together like cattle when Jaël's gaze caught mine. Jaël – a big-hearted, intelligent and graceful woman, mother of a sweet little boy called Ilay. She was very calm, although she had been separated from her son who was still so young. I didn't know what was going on. But, I had the impression, she did. As the train started to move she said calmly, "Sister Käthi, don't ever forget us." I don't know what happened to her. I think I don't want to know. But I will keep the promise I didn't say aloud. I have to be strong.'

I want to know what happened to Ilay. Käthi describes how she sent him via a camp in Rivesaltes to Banyuls-sur-Mer, where there is a young children's home also run by the Swiss Red Cross. She has heard from the carers there that he is doing very well physically, but nobody can tell what the psychological effects of being separated from his mother have been.

I stare blankly ahead, incapable of saying anything. A lump as tough as dried mashed potato sticks in my throat. I catch sight of the family in the distance. I hug Käthi, press my last bar of Cailler milk chocolate, which I had in my bag just in case, into her hand, and promise to stay in touch with her, even though I don't know how I will manage that. I get up and hurry in the direction of the grotto.

Lourdes ~ Saturday, 24 August 1940

From a priest, Madame learned that at nine o'clock every evening there is a procession of lights in devotion to the Virgin Mary. She didn't want to miss this and, as it is currently forbidden to be out after dark, we spontaneously decided to find accommodation last night.

The procession began at the podium opposite the grotto. The pilgrims carried a statue of Mary, lit candles and held them in their hands. Even the children were affected by the calm atmosphere and behaved very soberly. The Mysteries of the Rosary are prayed during the procession: on Saturdays, the Joyful Mysteries; on Tuesdays and Fridays, like yesterday, the Sorrowful Mysteries; on Sundays and Wednesdays the Glorious Mysteries; on Mondays and Thursdays the Luminous Mysteries. I prayed in German, not being familiar with the different rosary prayers in French. After the procession, at the Rosary Basilica, the pilgrims were blessed by bishops and priests. In the crowd I saw lots of people beaming with happiness, for whom the community experience seemed to be the most important thing and whose hearts had been set alight by an atmosphere charged with belief and confidence. I had to think of Käthi and of the countless people who have been far more directly affected by this war than I. Would I have the strength and courage to deal with this misery like Käthi?

Old Harbour, Biarritz ~ Sunday, 1 September 1940

The rain drums unstoppably on my open umbrella while I try to avoid the puddles so that my unsuitable shoes don't get completely ruined. The fishing boats are tightly moored in the Old Harbour, hidden behind its protective walls, yet bobbing wildly on the waves of the Bay of Biscay. I wonder if the fishermen went to sea this morning even in such a storm, to try their luck at returning with an abundant catch. The open sea flings huge waves angrily at the land. Only yesterday the waves were lapping gently in bright sunshine. The bizarre rock formations that rise out of the water defy the storm, seeming much more solid than they do in fine weather. My father always said that the power and strength of Nature makes people look small. How right he was!

Villa Kerlys, Biarritz ~
Sunday, 15 September 1940

Dear Lydia,

I am looking out of my bedroom window in Biarritz, in the South of France. My eyes glimpse the blue water and I think back to our Sunday trips to Lake Zug, where in fine weather we let both our souls and feet relax – the latter in the cool water – and talked about many things. Such lovely memories!

The confusion of war, which is bringing so much misery to Europe at the moment, has driven me and my employers out of Paris and into the South of France, from where it seems very far away. So far that I am even able to enjoy moments of happiness, such as when I look at the boundless-seeming Atlantic and feel myself to be on holiday. Of course I also have thoughts of the future and what will happen. I sometimes start brooding on such thoughts and feel myself a victim of the political machinations of big and important men, who dictate the lives of small citizens like us with their decisions and chess moves. When I manage not to think like this, I am happy in my daily life here. Working with the children gives me plenty to do and fills me with contentment. I don't want to do anything else.

I want to tell you about an interesting, thought-provoking encounter. On a recent walk along the beach promenade, a dapperly dressed man spoke to me in broken French and invited me to have coffee with him. I was quite taken aback. French men are usually very charming and by no means shy, but I have never been solicited so directly. I agreed and we soon sat down at a small bistro table, ordering coffee and *éclairs*. Robert – so he introduced himself – and I had a nice conversation, and I felt very attracted to his intelligent, forthcoming manner and his clear, blue eyes. He told me that he would be spending his holidays in this wonderful place. The longer we sat together, the more his German accent became noticeable and I was suddenly aware that I was playing with fire. I managed to excuse myself without him noticing how well I was able to speak his language. I spent the whole night worrying about how much I had told him of myself and whether that might have given me away. It's such a shame – the young man gave me real butterflies and I could sense that he has a good heart.

I hope that everything is very well with you. I look forward to hearing from you and send you my very best wishes.

Your French friend, Claire

Villa Kerlys, Biarritz ~
Sunday, 15 September 1940

Dear Käthi,

I hope that this letter from not-too-distant Biarritz reaches you. I managed to find the address of the Red Cross Distribution Centre in Toulouse and was told that the post for camps in the South of France is distributed from there.

It was a great pleasure to meet you in Lourdes. Your stories of your work moved me deeply and I would like to send you a small donation, so that you can buy something that is desperately needed. I find the suffering of the children, as you portrayed it, unbelievable. Although only a few kilometres away, I live in quite a different reality. Guilt about the fact that I am living very comfortably despite the war haunts me regularly.

I wish you strength for your undertakings and all the best from the bottom of my heart!

Yours, Claire Widmer

Biarritz ~ Monday, 21 October 1940

I would never have dared to dream that I might one day celebrate my birthday beside the sea. Madame gave me a beautiful silk scarf, which I am wearing now along with my sunglasses. Not around my neck, but draped lightly over my hair. I stroll along beside the sea with plans to treat myself to coffee and a piece of cake. The sun shines not only outside but also within me, as I think about my mistress' generosity. I pass the casino, aiming for the Grand Café. My heart stops for a second when I catch sight of Robert on the terrace of my favourite café. Immediately I raise my shoulders and hunch a little, as though this posture might make me invisible. Hoping that he hasn't seen me, I walk on. I am irritated by the fact that I no longer feel free here since meeting Robert. That he is still here seems suspicious to me. After all, the rendezvous at which he told me he would be spending his holidays here was more than a month ago. Strange.

Thursday, 7 November 1940

Blackout between 10pm and 6am is ordered in Switzerland, so that enemy planes won't be able to see the border.

Ligny-le-Ribault ~ Tuesday, 24 December 1940

The presents are considerably more modest than last year's. A turkey was nowhere to be found; the scarcity of meat makes itself felt even here. The little that one can get with ration coupons is not enough to live on. We are lucky that the farmsteads in the castle grounds provide some things such as eggs, milk and butter. Now and then – mainly for a special occasion – a chicken is slaughtered. In addition, Madame has her sources, from whom we can sometimes buy something. As well as money, cigarettes are a popular item for exchange. I find it unimaginable that a family could survive on the official food rations. Hunger would be guaranteed. Although we have to limit ourselves a lot, we definitely don't have to starve.

Now that the Germans have left the castle – I don't know why, as France is still occupied – we have returned to Bon-Hôtel. I found my documents untouched in the place where I had left them. I will keep them my whole life in memory of the anxiety that they caused. Or, rather, in memory of my forgetfulness.

I carefully wrap the little presents I bought in the South for the children, Monsieur and Madame in red tissue paper and try to tie bows. I succeed, but they don't look anything like as nice as the bows in the confectioner's in Biarritz from where I got the idea.

1941

Ligny-le-Ribault ~ Wednesday, 15 January 1941

Snow has been lying for weeks and it is bitingly cold. It takes a long time until the children have put on their woolly hats, gloves and jackets and are ready to go for a walk. It isn't very comfortable to be outside right now, even though Madame has loaned me her warm fur coat. On our walk we meet a farmer's wife, who has rented one of the farmsteads belonging to the castle. She complains about the bitter cold in the house, which due to the lack of coal and wood, prevails. Even the potatoes in the cellar are frozen. I feel for the thin woman, who has to take care of her farm and three children single-handedly since her husband was called up. The unlucky man was captured by the Germans and now has to work in a munitions factory in Germany. The farmer's wife says that she will send the few things she can spare by military post to Germany. Whether her husband will ever get the precious little parcel, she doesn't know.

Ligny-le-Ribault ~ Sunday, 2 February 1941

Every time Madame asks me to come to her I am nervous, although she only ever sets me tasks in a matter-of-fact, distant tone of voice and has never yet reprimanded me. Today she told me that it is currently taking a very long time for the Swiss legation to process visa applications and so I should start getting one for my annual holiday at Easter, which falls on 13 April this year, now.

If there's one thing I don't like, it's paperwork. But there's nothing to be done but set about it in the near future.

Swiss Embassy, Paris ~
Monday, 24 February 1941

Dear Miss Widmer,

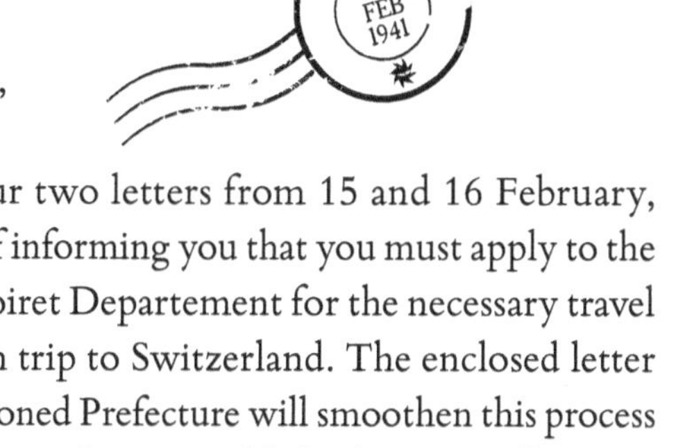

In reference to your two letters from 15 and 16 February, I have the honour of informing you that you must apply to the Prefecture of the Loiret Departement for the necessary travel pass for your return trip to Switzerland. The enclosed letter for the above-mentioned Prefecture will smoothen this process for you. It will, however, be very unlikely that you will receive this pass by 6 March. Additionally, you will have to request an exit visa from the Prefecture, which will be entered into your passport. You will find your passport enclosed; it has been extended to 23 May 1941 so that you have enough time to receive your travel pass.

Please be assured of my sincerest respect for you,

The Legation Councillor

Ligny-le-Ribault ~ Sunday, 2 March 1941

Overwhelmed, I look at the piece of paper lying in front of me. Madame seems to have been right – the process of getting a visa is really not easy at the moment. If I have understood everything correctly, I need to get both a travel pass and an exit visa in order to leave France. I don't like this exaggerated bureaucracy and yet I have no other option but to submit to the machine.

I hadn't noticed that my new passport was only valid for six months. It's fortunate that the gentlemen at the legation have a better eye for such things than I.

Ligny-le-Ribault ~
Friday, 2 May 1941

Dear Mr Legation Councillor,

I am writing in reference to your letter from 24 February, in which you kindly informed me that I would need to apply to the Prefecture of the Loiret Departement for a travel pass as well as the necessary *Visa de sortie de France*.

I did this without delay at the beginning of March, sending the required documents to the appropriate place.

As I have thus far received no answer, I would like to ask you if you have any news about my case.

I thank you in advance for your assistance.

Yours respectfully,

Claire Widmer

Swiss Legation, Paris ~
Saturday, 17 May 1941

Dear Miss Widmer,

I write in reference to your recent request for a *Laissez-passer*
to return to Switzerland. Unfortunately, I must inform you
that the formalities required for the issuance of such a document have been changed. One must now travel to Switzerland
through Germany. The possibility of returning to Switzerland
directly from the previously Free Zone no longer exists.

The border must be crossed at Elfringen in order to get into
Germany. The border crossing to Switzerland is in Basel.

You must therefore fill in all your documents and forms once
again. In addition, we require your valid passport, three photos
and your exact place of birth.

My sincerest wishes in this regard,
The Legation Councillor

Ligny-le-Ribault ~ Tuesday, 20 May 1941

Worn out. For nearly four months now I've been trying
to get a visa that will allow me to travel home for a short time.
I am beset by doubts that I will be able to travel to Switzerland
at all while this war continues. A strange and unexpected
feeling of homesickness creeps up on me. I had lulled myself
into a sense of security with the thought that I could get
onto a train any time and be in St. Gallen a few hours later,

and homesickness had never caught up with me. I was here
voluntarily, with the option of leaving immediately if I had
a convincing reason to. This new situation puts the whole
thing in a different light. I suddenly feel trapped, not knowing whether I will be able to see my family this year. The fact
that I can't travel directly from France to Switzerland makes
me particularly nervous. I have looked up Elfringen, which
is in the Moselle Departement in the North East, right on the
German border. I would have to take a detour and return
home via Germany. The thought of having to travel into
enemy territory is disturbing and scary. Who knows what
could happen there. What if I was arrested?

In addition, my emergency passport has expired. I wonder
if I should submit my old, still-valid passport, now that I've
found it again. Will anyone notice?

Les Sables-D'Olonne ~
Tuesday, 10 June 1941

Dear Countess,

I am pleased to be able to offer you two sunny rooms with
an ocean view.

The house is quiet and well maintained, in a good location
and very comfortable, as you will see from the photo on the
front of this card.

I hope to hear from you soon.

With sincerest regards, Elise Saigeau
Family Guesthouse Les Mouettes

Ligny-le-Ribault ~ Sunday, 15 June 1941

Madame is planning a holiday by the sea, I think, as I arrange the post on Madame's desk after happening to have met the postman by the castle gate and taking the letters in. Les Sables-D'Olonne – I have no idea on which coast the place is. I wonder whether I will still be here then or if I will be spending the holidays in Switzerland. Has Madame planned on having me there, or has she made other arrangements for the children's care in case I am able to travel? She doesn't show her cards in matters like these. We have now been at the castle for a good six months and I would really appreciate a change of scene. There's not really much for me to do here on my days off.

Consular Section, German Embassy, Paris ~ Saturday, 21 June 1941

Dear Miss Widmer,

You are kindly asked to fill out the three enclosed forms and return them together with three photographs of yourself.

The issuance of a permit from the authorities in Berlin may take five to six weeks.

On behalf of the Honorary Consul,
Albert Hohenegg

Ligny-le-Ribault ~ Tuesday, 1 July 1941

Two weeks ago the castle was occupied again. Today, the troops are leaving. They have been called to Russia, which has clearly agitated them. The Front is calling and, with it, the dull certainty that not all of their comrades will survive the campaign. It makes the otherwise confident officers seem vulnerable. They gather in the trophy room, writing letters to their loved ones and packing up souvenirs and personal items, like books, which they have come to possess over the last few months. Melancholically, they hand their letters to the military postman so that they can be sent home before their departure.

The regiment gathers in Ligny's market square. The officers and lieutenant who were billeted in the castle wear their field uniforms and call for their freshly shod horses straight away. They politely bid us farewell and ride towards the village centre. A little later they start to sing,

> *Arise, comrade! The time is ripe,*
>
> *The heavens are split by a fiery stripe.*
>
> *Let's wait no longer. We'll turn the propeller on!*
>
> *The infantry is calling, 'March forward!'*
>
> *Let's head for Russia, the Führer is calling.*
>
> *And so, my dear, adieu!*
>
> *The Eastern Army is storming to victory!*

Night gradually swallows the marching song. All is quiet. The stars glimmer softly.

St. Gallen ~ Friday, 25 July 1941

Tears of relief in my eyes, I start up the slope to my parents'
house as twilight falls. I have never been so happy to come
home. The journey was the most nerve-wracking I have ever
experienced. I can hardly believe that I was still in Paris this
morning. A Paris that has changed since our escape last June.
The sight of the red swastika flags, the German street signs
– Army Car Park, Air Force Hospital, Armed Forces High
Command Tyre Store – made me sad. It also seems that every
French person has swapped their car for a bicycle; there was
hardly a car to be seen on the streets.

If one thing was made clear to me on my journey,
which was peppered by countless checkpoints, it was this:
we are at war. More than once I thought my journey was
over. At every checkpoint fear panted down my neck like
a monster, even though I wasn't doing anything wrong and
had all the necessary papers with me. When I finally got
to the German-Swiss border and felt the end of my odyssey
approaching, my luggage was confiscated by German border
officials – apparently it will be returned to me after a routine inspection. After all the inspections and questions I was
happy to simply be able to pass and left all my possessions,
including those precious items associated with my French life,
with the German border officials. With only my handbag,
in which are the important travel permit and my passport,
amongst other things, I open the familiar, skewed red gate
to my parents' house.

Ligny-le-Ribault ~
Sunday, 3 August 1941

Dear Miss Claire,

Time flies by – over a week has passed since your departure.
We received your postcard of the beautiful little town of St.
Gallen. All of us were very happy to hear from you.

If you would like, you may extend your holidays until Friday,
29 August. The children are well; I am always with them.
They do miss you very much, though.

We all hope you have a wonderful holiday! Best wishes to your
whole family!

The de Maraberry family

St. Gallen ~ Thursday, 7 August 1941

Georg came home unexpectedly on leave from the Front.
Equally unexpectedly, he hugged me when he arrived – something that he has never done – and shortly afterwards asked me
to go for a walk. We talked for a long time: he about his time
in the army and me about my experiences in France, especially
my dramatic journey and the snappy officials at the border. When
I was finished with my stories, he was quiet for a long time,
looked at me earnestly and said, 'Klara, I beg you, stay here.'

I was silent for just as long as my brother and then wanted
to know why I should stay. As opposed to me, he understands

politics and is convinced that the French occupiers' attitude has become tougher in recent months, that the Germans will let their influence be felt even in the officially unoccupied South, that the Vichy government is becoming a farce and that the war will not be over soon. The global situation is unpredictable. The Führer to the north of our border is said to be simply mad and capable of anything. One hears awful things from all over Europe – unimaginable horrors are taking place. People are not just dying at the Front; tens of thousands of Jews are being deported and gassed: women, men, the elderly, children. Jaël flashed suddenly through my mind, but Georg carried on talking.

Critics of the regime are being shot on sight or hanged, people are starving, men in occupied regions are having to work in terrible conditions as forced labour in the Germans' military factories, regularly dying of exhaustion. Already awfully exploited, occupied countries are expected to supply the German army with scarce goods and war payments. 'Yes, Klara,' he finished, bringing his factual explanation to a close in his usual quiet, succinct and intelligent way, 'that's how it is in Europe.'

My head is spinning. I wonder how Georg knows all this. And why I, who have been there, haven't noticed anything. I feel miserable. With a few exceptions, I had been having the time of my life!

Even though I don't want to admit it, Georg's request comforts me. The terrifying experiences of my journey are still all too present in my mind. At the same time I feel awful, because I love France and the children.

Unexpectedly, I hear myself saying, 'Georg, I'll stay. But from now on, please call me Claire.'

Basel ~ Monday, 11 August 1941

Dear Miss Widmer,

Enclosed you will find the report on your luggage together with the key for your suitcase. Please collect it from the station in St. Gallen in order to avoid any storage costs.

With my best wishes,
The Commissioner for Repatriation

Swiss War Welfare Office

Basel ~ Tuesday, 12 August 1941

Dear Miss Widmer,

The matter detailed in your letter from 11 August 1941 had already been dealt with before it arrived. The expenses are as follows:

Cargo Strasbourg – Basel (German Railways)   Fr. 5.70

Cargo Basel (German Railways) – St. Gallen   Fr. 6.75

Ticket Basel – St. Gallen   Fr. 7.50

Total   Fr. 19.95

If this sum is not too much, please use the enclosed deposit form to pay the outstanding amount to the Post Office account of Artur Oettinger-Meili in Basel.

Respectfully yours,
The Commissioner for Repatriation

Swiss War Welfare Office

St. Gallen ~ Thursday, 14 August 1941

My walk to the post office is not a light one. I have never found it so difficult to write one – or rather two – letters. With a heavy heart I wrote to Monsieur Deschamps that in the current circumstances I will not be able to return to Bon-Hôtel after my holidays. I also provided him with as much information as possible, as I know how hungry for knowledge he is and how difficult it is to get news from France at the moment.

I have enclosed a letter for Madame, in which above all I want to thank her for the extremely good position that she was able to offer me. I then wrote a few lines for each child, in order to give each of them a personal message. I hope very much that they will be able to understand my decision. Secretly, I hope that we will one day see each other again.

Since promising Georg to stay in Switzerland, I have lain awake every night thinking about my intuitive decision. For a whole week I couldn't find it in me to take the finished letters to the post office. If there is one thing I don't want, it's to disappoint Monsieur Deschamps. But now the whole thing is final and cannot be undone.

Along with the letter I am carrying twenty francs and the deposit form, in order to pay the costs of my repatriation. A chapter of my life is closing: the best so far. I am sad.

Boncourt ~
Saturday, 16 August 1941

My dear Claire,

I was very surprised this morning to receive your letter of the 14th from St. Gallen along with the additional correspondence for my daughter, which I will forward at the next possible opportunity.

I had had no idea that you had undertaken to return to Switzerland, but was happy to read that you had got home safely.

You didn't tell me whether Bon-Hôtel Castle has been occupied again or whether the occupiers have carried off many things. That would interest me a great deal. In the future we will send food packages according to the suggestions you gave us. Regarding the First Holy Communion dress, I am not yet sure if it will be possible to send this. We will try to get permission.

As you probably know, I had been hoping to return to Paris for certain matters of business and to go from there to Bon-Hôtel

Castle. Having received no answer to my application, I must assume that this has been denied. I will try to go there in October, but I know that it is becoming ever more difficult. Nevertheless, there is a glimmer of hope that I will succeed.

I thank you for the precious help that you gave my daughter and send my best wishes to you, my dear Claire, as well as to your dear mother.

Henry Deschamps

P.S. I would be glad to have a conversation with you. Mrs Deschamps is going to Bad Ragaz tomorrow, where she will spend two or three weeks at Hotel Hof Ragaz. I will spend Sunday, 24 August with her and will be in Zurich on the afternoon of the 25th and morning of the 26th. If this journey would give me the chance to meet with you, I would be very happy.

St. Gallen ~ Wednesday, 20 August 1941

The snowy white hand embroidery of the First Holy Communion dress glides smoothly through my fingers. Before my return I had asked Julius, who since Father's death has been carrying out the few commissions for hand embroidery, to embroider a First Holy Communion dress. My mother had then sewn it up and I had planned to bring this unique item back from holiday with me as a present for Madeleine, who will receive her First Holy Communion in the autumn. And if I now can't be there myself, I want my little girl to at least be able to wear this dress for the event.

Boncourt ~
Friday, 22 August 1941

My dear Claire,

This morning I received your letter of the 20th. I have a clash, as on Monday, 25 August I have to be in Zurich Seebach at 2pm. I therefore would like to ask if it would be possible for you to leave St. Gallen earlier – at 9:54, for example – so that you would be in Zurich at 11:12.

You could go straight to the Second Class station restaurant on the first floor, and tell the hostess to direct me to Mademoiselle Widmer when I ask for you.

Tomorrow I will be travelling to the Grand Hotel Hof Ragaz in Ragaz, where I will be meeting Madame Deschamps and Mademoiselle Marcelle.

I don't yet know whether I will be leaving Ragaz at seven o'clock on Monday morning, in which case I would arrive in Zurich at 8:38. If so, I will of course wait on the platform for the arrival of your train at 11:12. If I only leave Ragaz at 9:52, I will arrive in Zurich at 11:20 and come straight to the station restaurant to meet you. We could eat together and talk during the meal. If you are pressed for time, you could take the train back to St. Gallen at 13:38, or alternatively at 15:55 or 18:05, as it suits you.

If I don't hear anything to the contrary, I will be at Zurich station restaurant on Monday morning at 11:25.

I am very much looking forward to hearing your news in detail. Please pass on my best wishes to Mrs Widmer.

Warmest wishes,
Henry Deschamps

P.S. If possible, I will telephone you from Ragaz tomorrow evening or on Sunday, to make sure that everything is all right for you.

Zurich ~ Monday, 25 August 1941

It's only a few steps from the station restaurant to the world-famous Zurich Bahnhofstrasse. Seeing as I have time, I decide to make the most of the afternoon and take a walk through the biggest of Switzerland's cities. The bright light of the afternoon sun makes me put on my sunglasses as I leave the ticket hall. The meeting with Monsieur Deschamps has left me feeling relieved and grateful that he doesn't hold a grudge against me or my decision. He, his wife and his daughter are sad that I won't be taking up my position again; according to him, they were very satisfied with my work. But they are also aware of current world events and know what uncertain times we are living in.

While we enjoyed our Zurich veal ragout with rösti – Monsieur had insisted that I order this expensive delicacy – and drank a glass of red wine, I told him all the details of the last few weeks in France. When I left Bon-Hôtel it had not been occupied again. But apparently Monsieur has since come into possession of the information that this is sadly the case again. Georg, it occurred to me, had been right in his assessment of the situation.

I explained how supply chains have got worse in the last few weeks, that many of our previous sources of food had dried up for reasons unknown to me. Monsieur replied that he was currently trying to find new ways of sending food and other items to his daughter and her family. He seems to have been able to recruit a middleman who maintains hiding places in the house for employees of the castle. He smuggles the goods in hay bales on a cart, hides them in the house and then brings the precious items to the castle when an opportunity presents itself. An undertaking that is not entirely free of risk, it seems to me. But what are the alternatives in times like these?

Monsieur Deschamps is a man who impresses me, I think, as I reach the famous Parade Square. His generosity, warmth and heartfelt nature indicate a fine character. Despite his successful career as a businessman and politician, he is uncompromising in putting his family first. It's an attitude that seems to have been forgotten by many people these days.

Grand Hotel Hof Ragaz, Bad Ragaz ~
Wednesday, 27 August 1941

Dear Miss Widmer,

Thank you very much for sending me the dress, which I was very pleased to receive. The St. Gallen lace is of outstanding quality and the dress very prettily made. I am sure that Madeleine will look like an angel in it.

Our daughter misses you very much. Every day I pray that she has found someone to take care of the children. Mr Deschamps told me everything that you discussed with him. I also have some news from over there. How terrible this war is for the countless souls who must suffer!

With my best wishes,
Bernadette Deschamps

Boncourt ~ Thursday, 28 August 1941

My dear Claire,

I was very pleased to see you and to receive news from Bon-Hôtel, even if it wasn't of the best sort. On the day after our meeting we received a letter from the Countess, dated 13 August.

She asked for any news of your journey and told us that we can't imagine what anxiety your departure had caused her and that the whole household is sorrowful. She added that you are a girl of immense capability and that she will never forget you.

To thank you for your extraordinary service to our family, we would like to pay you your normal wages for the month of August. You will find enclosed 100 francs, which I had previously been sending to Mrs Widmer.

My daughter has requested a letter from you. I think that she must now be in possession of the letter that I had forwarded to her.

She also told me that Jean is convinced that you will return. He continuously says, 'Nanny is in Paris to visit her mama.' Madeleine is mired in sadness and can hardly be cheered up.

I must emphasize, my dear Claire, how unbelievably grateful I am for everything that you have done for my daughter and grandchildren.

After everything that you told me, I do not think that you can return to Bon-Hôtel Castle in the coming months and will endeavour to find someone to replace you.

Thank you very much again that you took the trouble to meet me in Zurich.

My very best wishes, dear Claire,
Henry Deschamps

St. Gallen ~ Friday, 12 September 1941

I carefully remove the tape emblazoned with the words 'Roger Gallet' from the rustling tissue paper that is wrapped around the precious, round soap. The smell of roses reminds me of my France and I only use it very sparingly. Shortly before my departure I had bought five of them, all finely scented with rose. I had actually intended them as presents, but when it was clear that I wouldn't be able to return, I kept them all for myself in the hope of being able to conserve a piece of France. Madame only ever used products from this traditional Master Perfumer. She had told me that these timeless classics, made with excellent craftsmanship and attention to detail, are ordered by royal courts around the world.

St. Gallen ~ Autumn 1941

Dear Miss Widmer,

We have the pleasure of cordially inviting you, as a Swiss repatriate, to become an active member of our society.

This society unites repatriated comrades from the cantons of St. Gallen, Appenzell and Thurgau, and is concerned with providing advice and defending your interests before the authorities and society. It is part of the National Society for the Union of Swiss Repatriates, which represents all parts of the country with its 21 branches and approx. 6,000 members.

Only through working together can each individual be strong enough to prevail in these difficult times. Accordingly, please send the enclosed membership registration as soon as possible to the President of our society: David Gähler, Oberstrasse 16, St. Gallen.

You are also warmly invited to attend our weekly meetings at Marktplatz restaurant every Tuesday evening. The monthly fee is 50 rappen (not required from the unemployed or those without financial means). As an active member you will receive our free 'Information Sheet' every month and can enjoy all the benefits of a friendly society.

Your humble servant,
The Actuary of the Society for Swiss Repatriates, East Switzerland Group

St. Gallen ~ Tuesday, 21 October 1941

After two birthdays in Paris, I am celebrating this one – my 23rd – at home again. I don't feel like celebrating; at the moment I feel completely in abeyance, considered to be a Swiss repatriate and, what's more, unemployed. The feeling of not knowing what the future has in store for me is a strange one! My family's relief about my return is enormous, my guilt towards Madame equally so.

I often think of my French family and cannot rid myself of the gloomy feeling that I have abandoned Madame and the children in this difficult situation. I haven't had any news of them for several weeks and the thought that the children will be gradually forgetting me – and, indeed, that I have probably been replaced by now – cuts me to the quick.

Even though there is a never-ending amount of work to do at home, I am bored. I am currently helping out everywhere it is required, be it in the embroidery workshop or around

the house. I need to accept the fact that I will have to find
a job here.

Boncourt ~
Tuesday, 9 December 1941

My dear Claire,

I am happy to be able to tell you that I have received news
from Paris from two or three different sources, albeit without
great detail.

We know that the Countess gave birth to a son on 13 November
and that on 25 November she and the child were doing well.
The christening was expected to take place last Thursday or on
the Thursday before. Mrs Marie-Louise and Count Ramolino
are the godparents. The baby has been named Antoine.

That is unfortunately all that I am able to tell you. I was
supposed to travel to Paris on 22 November and had received
my identity card, but was delayed by important meetings and
a session of the National Council. Still, I anticipate being
able to travel on 10 or 15 January. Mrs Deschamps also
hopes to receive permission to visit Bon-Hôtel in January
or February. We will of course send you news upon our
return.

Mrs Marie-Thérèse came to visit us in the middle of October
with Yseult. Unfortunately we weren't able to profit from
her visit all that much, as she had to be back in Paris on 31
October at the latest.

The uncertainty of not knowing when or whether one will see one's loved ones again is one of the greatest challenges of our time, I find. Material restrictions can be borne, but deprivations of the soul gnaw at everyone.

With my best wishes, dear Claire,
Henry Deschamps

St. Gallen ~
Friday, 12 December 1941

Dear Monsieur Deschamps,

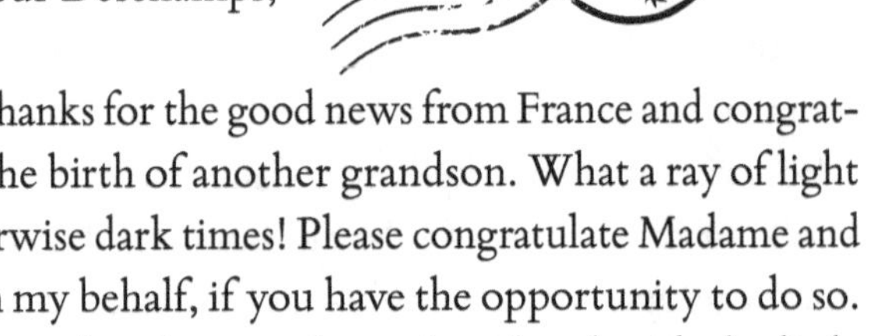

My deepest thanks for the good news from France and congratulations on the birth of another grandson. What a ray of light in these otherwise dark times! Please congratulate Madame and Monsieur on my behalf, if you have the opportunity to do so. I am sending enclosed a coverlet embroidered with the little boy's initials and hope that it will find its way to Antoine.

I also wondered if you might have the chance to send a Christmas parcel to the castle from me? Being able to send the children a small present is a matter very dear to me.

There is not much news from me. I have sent several applications for jobs as a kindergarten teacher here in East Switzerland, thus far without any positive result. It seems that not many positions are open.

My best wishes to you and your wife,
Claire Widmer

Boncourt ~ Friday, 19 December 1941

My dear Claire,

Upon returning from my travels I found your letter together
with correspondence from my friend from Orléans, Mr de
Charsonville. He was recently able to telephone Bon-Hôtel
to get the latest news. The Countess was still in bed (this must
have been on 1 or 2 December), but the nanny reported that
the birth had gone well, Antoine is a big boy and that he and
his mother are doing well. Everything, then, is as well as it
can be; we hope and pray that it will continue so.

I am very keen to meet my eleventh grandchild and am therefore doing my utmost to be able to travel to Bon-Hôtel Castle
on 15/20 January. I will not fail to pass on your messages to my
daughter and her children, who will no doubt be delighted
to hear from you.

Please don't take the trouble of sending a Christmas parcel;
you need to have permission to do that. I have already used all
the permissions that I received and despatched all the mail for
the month of December. I will not, however, fail to convey
your tender wished to Bon-Hôtel.

You told me that you haven't yet found a suitable position.
If we are able to help you in this regard, you hopefully know
that we would be glad to do so.

Mrs Grandchamp's little Françoise is with us, probably until
the end of January. As of the day before yesterday, Mrs Joseph

and her six-month-old daughter, who is so sweet and pretty, are also staying with us.

Please be assured of my warmest wishes, dear Claire, and we wish you a merry Christmas and a happy New Year.

Henry Deschamps

St. Gallen ~
Saturday, 20 December 1941

My dear Lydia,

A long time has passed since last we heard from one another. I hope that you and your loved ones are well. I wish you a peaceful and merry Christmas from – probably against all expectations – St. Gallen, to where I returned in the summer. As for many people, this is also a difficult time for me. The highly unstable situation in France meant that it wasn't possible for me to return to my job after my annual holiday at home. Since then my heart has been divided: on the one hand, I am thankful to be able to live in peace here in Switzerland, but on the other I miss my life in Paris and, above all, the children.

I hope that the New Year will bring peace for us all. On this note, I embrace you affectionately,

Your Claire

1942

Boncourt ~
Monday, 26 January 1942

My dear Claire,

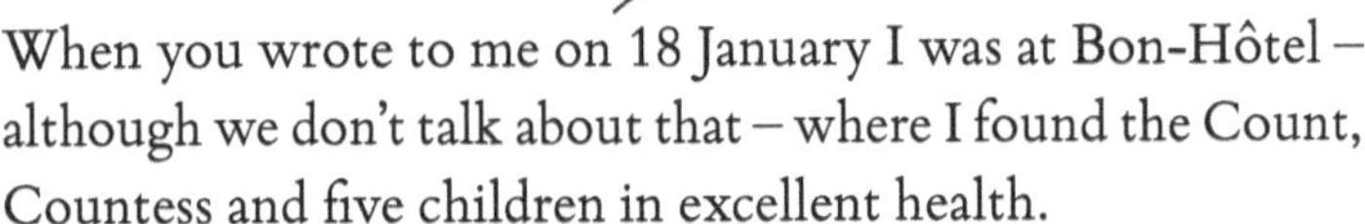

When you wrote to me on 18 January I was at Bon-Hôtel –
although we don't talk about that – where I found the Count,
Countess and five children in excellent health.

All of them asked for news about you.

Little Antoine was, as previously reported, born on 13
November. His mother had jaundice afterwards but is now
well again. Unfortunately Madame Marie-Thérèse is not
happy with the nanny whom she has had for eight or ten
days, and so she is looking for another one.

The Count is doing well. Eight days ago we went on a two-
hour walk together, which would have been unthinkable
a short while ago on account of his leg. The castle is no longer
occupied and nor are the estates in the neighbourhood.

Up until now there were no catering problems at Bon-Hôtel;
there is milk and enough butter, but absolutely no meat except
for rabbit and occasional poultry. A sheep was slaughtered for
my visit and there are now two or three left…

I don't need to tell you how much you are missed. Jean couldn't
understand why I hadn't brought you with me. He is, however,
doing very well and is truly sweet. Madeleine has started to eat
better; Aurélie is always a little confused and absent – she isn't

growing and is too thin for a nearly five-year-old. Paulette is very well. If it hadn't been so cold, I would probably have brought Madeleine back to Switzerland with me.

I returned on Saturday evening and had visitors for the whole day yesterday, but I wanted to send this news to you as quickly as possible.

I send you, my dear Claire, my best wishes.

Henry Deschamps

St. Gallen ~
Saturday, 31 January 1942

Dear Miss Widmer,

We received your esteemed address from Miss Margrit Ehrenbolger. For several years she taught crafts to both our schoolchildren and, in a different capacity, older children. Unfortunately Frau Ehrenbolger, to our great regret, can no longer carry out her classes for reasons of health.

We are looking for a kindergarten teacher who would be pre-pared to teach crafts to the schoolchildren here in the home every other Friday evening, from 6pm to 8pm or from 5.30pm to 7.30pm, in return for compensation. The school has a small supply of the most common materials.

We would like to politely ask you if you might find it possible to take over the teaching of these classes?

We await your esteemed answer and remain respectfully yours,

Sister Hedy Bresch

Pear Tree Nursing School
St. Gallen East

St. Gallen ~ Monday, 2 February 1942

I have been looking for a job in Switzerland for many long
months and, now that I have found something, several doors
are opening. I have to decline Sister Bresch's job offer as I will
be starting my new job in Lucerne next week. I am swapping
the Seine for the Reuss, the sea for Lake Lucerne, the castle for
a confectioner's. But my duties will be the same and so I am
happy – I love working with children. In Central Switzerland
I will be responsible to look after the three children of the
Zemp family, who run a well known confectioner's and coffee
house. My love of pastries is well known and so a confectioner's doesn't seem to me a bad place to work. In addition, I will
be near to my old training college in Cham and to Lydia, who
teaches in Zug. So far, so good.

Zug ~ Tuesday, 10 February 1942

My dear Klara
(or should I say Claire?),

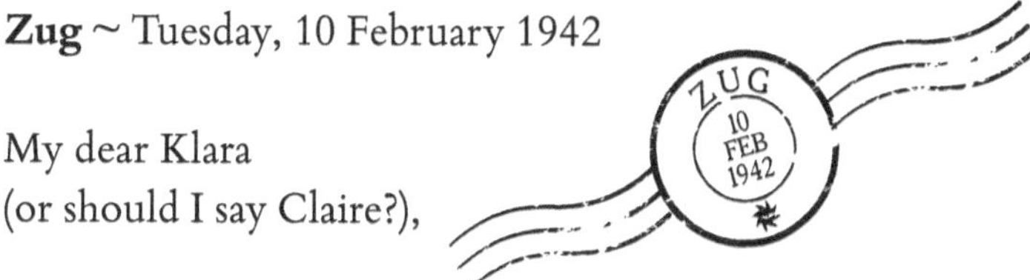

I was so happy to receive your message. Please forgive my late
reply, but I had a lot of work to do in January and so didn't
get round to writing to you.

I have often thought of you and wondered why you didn't
reply to my last letter, which I sent to the castle. I thought
a lot about where you could have fled. Simply not replying
for no reason is not in your character. I was worried about
you and missed our regular correspondence.

I can very imagine that the abrupt change from an elite life
in France to the middle class in little St. Gallen was quite
drastic. Times are certainly not easy and it might be that in the
current situation you will have to make compromises as far
as a new job is concerned. The dark clouds that are currently
hanging over Europe will one day disappear. And we are still
young. So don't let yourself be forced into doing something
that doesn't please you. I am thinking, for example, of something as final as marriage…

So far, everything is as good as it can be where I am concerned.
I am happy being a kindergarten teacher in Zug and am not planning to change anything about my situation in the near future.

On this note, my dear friend, relieved greetings.
Your Lydia

Boncourt ~
Wednesday, 4 March 1942

My dear Claire,

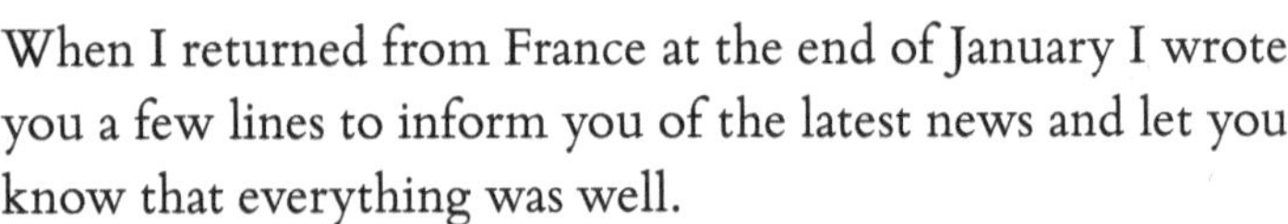

When I returned from France at the end of January I wrote you a few lines to inform you of the latest news and let you know that everything was well.

Today I received a letter from Bon-Hôtel dated 2 February. My daughter writes that she was unable to retain the new nanny, as she really didn't meet the standards of the household. She adds, 'If Claire would like to return, the position is open and will always remain so for her. You can gladly tell her that.' I am pleased to pass this on to you.

Madame Deschamps applied for a visa at the start of last month. She hopes that she will get the visa within fourteen days and would then spend two weeks in Paris and at Bon-Hôtel. She must, however, travel via Basel, Offenburg, Strasbourg and Nancy.

I hope that you are getting on well in Lucerne and send you, my dear Claire, my best wishes.

Henry Deschamps

Lucerne ~ Friday, 6 March 1942

I let my gaze slide over the millpond-still surface of Lake Lucerne, which lies embedded between high peaks before me. A swan swims by, cackling, and steals a piece of bread that someone has thrown in the lake from under a duck's nose. Its long neck gives it the advantage.

A month of hard work in Lucerne has flown by; I will be employed here for another four weeks and then have nothing to do again. Or not, if I accept the offer from Boncourt. I toy seriously with the idea of travelling to France again. I am certain that Monsieur Deschamps wouldn't send me back to Bon-Hôtel if it would put me in acute danger. Doesn't everything happen for a reason, even if we sometimes can't comprehend it in the here and now? Deep in my heart I know the answer that I will give Monsieur Deschamps.

Boncourt ~
Monday, 9 March 1942

My dear Claire,

I received your letter from the 6th of this month and we — Madame Deschamps and I — are incredibly pleased that you are available and willing to return to Bon-Hôtel.

I am of course unable to tell you if you will receive the necessary papers with ease, but as I will be in Bern next Monday evening, 16 March, for the National Council, I can visit the German Embassy on the following morning. It would be extremely helpful if I were able to take your passport with me. Would you therefore be willing to send it to me by next Friday at the latest? I will write to the Countess today and ask her to enquire about the procedure at the German command in Paris d'Orléans, so that your application – which will have to be sent from Bern to Berlin and then from Berlin to Paris – will be approved and processed without delay. You would therefore be in with a chance of having your visa issued at the end of April or, at the latest, in the first days of May.

It makes me very happy to think how much joy the news of your probable return will bring to my daughter and the children.

On this note, dear Claire, I send you my best wishes.

Henry Deschamps

Boncourt ~ Monday, 16 March 1942

Dear Miss Widmer,

Mr Deschamps received your letter and passport when he returned from his trip on Saturday evening. He will take the documents with him when he travels to Bern, in order to take them to the German Embassy (Légation d'Allemagne). He asked me to bring to your attention the fact that your passport expired at the start of September, if I am not mistaken.

Mrs Deschamps, who tried to get a visa to travel to Paris and Bon-Hôtel, did not receive one, as the German authorities did not view her motives for the journey as sufficiently valid. Mr Deschamps thinks that he will be able to inform you at the end of this week or middle of next how his visit to the German Embassy regarding your return to France went.

As you have not provided us with your address in Lucerne, we must continue to send letters to your address in St. Gallen.

Please accept my best wishes,
M. Wehrer – Secretary

Ligny-le-Ribault/Lucerne ~
Wednesday, 18 March 1942

The area of the swimming lake that I can make out through the thin branches is calm and still. But the whooping, shrieking and splashing comes without a doubt from that direction. I amble slowly onwards and am astonished to see that even in the afternoon there is still dew on the clover leaves in the verge. The sun hasn't yet been able to dry the leaves on this spring day – the high trees' leafy canopy is too thick. A happy shout rends the air – I look back at the lake just in time to see a naked man take a great leap from the jetty into the cold water, accompanied by his companions' cheers. Only their heads are visible above the water. I am touched by embarrassment yet cannot look away as the next young man climbs out of the water. His naked, white behind moves quickly towards the jetty; as he makes to turn around I nevertheless close my eyes. A new, dull splashing tells me that the well-built young man has landed in the water. A happy, relaxed crowd. And handsome, young men.

I wonder whether the Belgian nuns from the next-door property are genuinely angry when they encounter the naked German officers on their innocent walks with their protégés, or if they don't sneak a few glances in the direction of the alabaster bodies while covering the children's eyes.

I let myself sink into the damp grass, the blades pricking me through the thin fabric of my summer skirt. The bathing session comes to an end. As the men swim to shore to climb out, I let my upper body sink backwards so as not to be discovered. But my back doesn't touch the ground and I am falling and falling – into nothingness. As I open my eyes in shock, I find myself staring at the ceiling of my bedroom in Lucerne.

Boncourt ~
Tuesday, 24 March 1942

My dear Claire,

As agreed, last week I stopped by the German Embassy (Légation d'Allemagne) in Bern to present your case.

I was told that one should expect to wait two months for an answer and was given the four enclosed documents. Please fill them out carefully and emphasize the fact that Countess de Maraberry wishes to employ you again, facilitated by her father, Mr Henry Deschamps, National Council, and that you have already worked for my daughter looking after the four children from this date to that.

Mention also that the Countess is expecting her sixth child and cannot find anyone qualified to replace you.

You will have noticed that you have to supply four photos along with the documents.

As you have a domicile in St. Gallen, I would warmly recommend you to visit the German Embassy to present your case and submit the four relevant documents along with your current passport, which I am returning to you along with this letter.

You could also turn to the German Consulate in Lucerne, but as they will be leaving the city on 4 April it would be preferable if you would go to the Consulate in St. Gallen.

As regards the renewal of your passport, I am not certain if it is possible to add extra pages or if you will need to apply for a new one.

As soon as you have been to the German Embassy in St. Gallen, I would be grateful if you could let me know. I am curious to find out what they tell you and if you are hopeful or not.

I wish you a happy Easter and send you my best wishes, my dear Claire.

Henry Deschamps

St. Gallen ~
Friday, 10 April 1942

Dear Mr Deschamps,

I hope that you and the whole family had a good Easter.

My two months in Lucerne are already a thing of the past and since last week I have been back in St. Gallen. With reference to your thorough descriptions, first of all, I took care of my passport; it seems that I will need to apply for a new one, which, is not too complicated, as I already possess such a document. I immediately applied for a new one and was told that I should receive the new identity document in three weeks.

According to the German Embassy in St. Gallen – which I visited another day – I can only submit my visa application when I am in possession of the new passport with the applicable number. I have already prepared the four documents and required photos, so that as soon as I receive my passport I can submit everything and keep you informed of the developments in this case.

In the meantime I remain with best wishes,

Claire Widmer

Boncourt ~
Friday, 24 April 1942

My dear Claire,

I found your letter of 10 April waiting for me upon my return
from Bon-Hôtel, to which I had returned unexpectedly.

I was on business in Geneva when I received a telephone call
informing me that I was to be in France the following morning. Fortunately I had my passport with me and everything
went well.

My daughter was able to find a nanny in France – more accu-
rately in Sologne – who is good and with whom she is happy.
Nevertheless she would take you back straight away; my
daughter and the children would be happy if you were with
them again. All of them are very well and the children were
charming to me, especially Aurélie. I took a small walk alone
with Jean; he is very lively. Little Antoine, whom you don't
yet know, is growing magnificently. Paulette is a big girl and
Madeleine is always charming.

Each one of them tasked me with sending you thousands
of good wishes, including Miss Inelle Crinon, who currently
has to spend fourteen days in Paris with Paulette due to her
breathing problems.

During my stay we took photos. When I receive the prints,
I will send them to you. Life is continuing relatively easily
thanks to the farms in Haute-Métairie and Bouchaut. There

is always enough milk, butter and eggs. No one is occupying Bon-Hôtel or the region any more.

The Count has found a job in Paris, but he has to travel a lot, even on Saturday afternoons, and thanks to travel difficulties can rarely come to the castle.

The Countess intends to get a visa for the summer in order to travel with the children to the Free Zone. We are currently investigating whether she would have the opportunity to come here for three or four weeks.

Before I close, I would like to ask you to not speak to anyone of my trips to Bon-Hôtel Castle. I will tell you the reason for my visits in person.

As soon as you have news about your passport, I would be grateful if you could let me know.

Please accept my best wishes, dear Claire.

Henry Deschamps

St. Gallen ~ Sunday, 10 May 1942

'Refused!' With this single word, the clerk at the German Embassy shoves my documents and passport back at me. I stare at him aghast – he had barely looked at my visa application before throwing it out. I don't know whether he is even allowed to approve applications or not, but I am not brave enough to ask. With an almost unbeatable arrogance he turns away from me and begins shuffling a pile of papers. His stony look makes me shudder and almost takes my breath away. I feel immediately uneasy.

One word was enough to bury my confidence about the future. Cast down, I shuffle my documents back together, put everything neatly into my bag and leave the embassy building.

Boncourt ~
Saturday, 23 May 1942

My dear Claire,

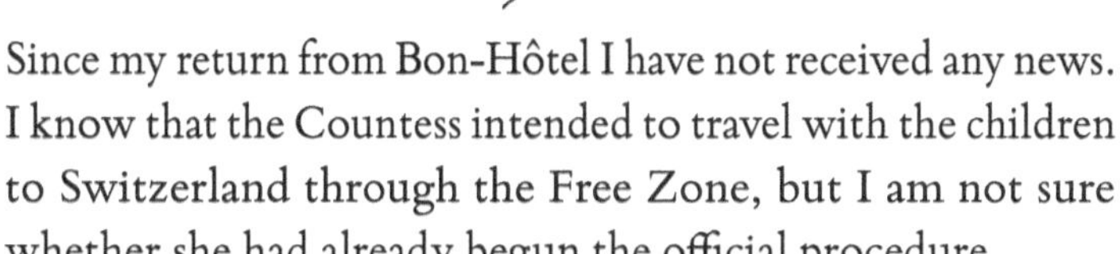

Since my return from Bon-Hôtel I have not received any news. I know that the Countess intended to travel with the children to Switzerland through the Free Zone, but I am not sure whether she had already begun the official procedure.

I am not surprised that the German Consulate told you it would be impossible to return to the Occupied Zone. If the Countess can come here with the children, though, you could still come to Boncourt for a visit, if you have time.

I have once again taken measures to travel to Bon-Hôtel. If nothing untoward happens, I will leave Boncourt on 13 or 14 June in order to be at Bon-Hôtel on the 16th. I will return to Switzerland on 28 or 29 June.

I will not fail to pass on your messages to my daughter, Mademoiselle Crinon and the five children. I do not know if Madame Deschamps will be able to accompany me. As you have experienced, it is difficult to get the necessary permits at the moment. Between us, however, it is not impossible. We have once again applied for a visa for my wife in France, but I do not yet dare to hope for a positive outcome.

I advise you to submit your documents to the German Embassy in writing. Sometimes stubbornness pays off.

I send you, dear Claire, my best wishes and greetings.
Henry Deschamps

Bern ~ Monday, 13 July 1942

Dear Miss Widmer,

We write in reference to your offer of service as a kindergarten teacher and your interview and discussion with us here in Bern on 8 July.

We are in agreement with a starting salary of 100 francs along with free board and laundry and, in the event of satisfaction with your services, will raise this accordingly.

We would like you to start on Monday, 27 July 1942. Please would you be so kind as to confirm your agreement?

We thank you for your efforts and hope that our professional relationship will be agreeable to both parties.

Yours sincerely, Gerber-Tobler

Aboard a train to Boncourt ~ Saturday, 25 July 1942

My brown leather suitcase has already seen a lot, I think, heaving it onto the luggage rack in my train compartment. I am leaving St. Gallen once again, eventful days before me. My journey will take me first of all to Boncourt in Jura, where I will see Madame, the children and Monsieur and Madame Deschamps again. Even though I am deeply saddened that a return to my French family doesn't seem to be possible, I am looking forward to spending two days with them. I am excited to see how the children have grown – after all, a year has passed since my departure from Bon-Hôtel. And children grow at such a fast pace that one only really notices when one doesn't see them every day. I will also finally get to meet the youngest family member, Antoine, who at eight months is no longer a newborn. I am excited.

After the weekend I will travel directly from Boncourt to Bern, which is not too far away, to take up my new position as a kindergarten teacher. I do not know in great detail what awaits me; I am to establish an in-house kindergarten for a mid-sized company and then lead it. Apart from during my studies, I have never worked as a kindergarten teacher in the classic sense of the word; I am excited and also somewhat nervous to see how I will master the work. At the same time I will have the opportunity of getting to know our capital city better. Thus far I have only been there twice and barely had time to see anything of the town, as I was either travelling through or, most recently, having an interview with Patron Gerber.

Aboard a train to Bern ~ Monday, 27 July 1942

My heart is filled with nostalgia. I feel like I have left a piece of it behind me. I spent the time almost exclusively with the children, who were so unbelievably happy to see me again that it made me emotional. They clung to me the entire weekend, but I didn't mind in the slightest. We played, sang, drew, exercised and then our time was already up and another farewell hung over us like the Sword of Damocles. I left very early this morning, yet all the children were already awake and with tearful voices begged me to remain, which I would have gladly done. But unfortunately this was not an option and so I am now sitting on a train that will have me in Bern in two hours.

I had the impression that Madame was also pleased to see her children happy and carefree. She must have enjoyed the peace. Her sixth pregnancy doesn't seem to be going unnoticed in these times of war and uncertainty.

I found it all the more difficult to say farewell when I realized that even the always optimistic and confident Mr Deschamps had resigned himself as far as permissions to enter and stay in France are concerned – at least for the moment. At supper he said that it is unlikely to change as long as the war lasts. It was wise of me to get myself a job in Switzerland, even though he would have preferred it otherwise.

Shortly before Bern I notice that my heart is not just partly but mainly in Boncourt. At this moment I have absolutely no idea how I am to enter my new position in a professional manner in just a few hours.

Bern ~ Wednesday, 21 October 1942

Another year is over – so now I have 24 years to my name!
The last three months were full of work and time has flown
by. I have become accustomed to my new tasks, even though
it is somewhat different to all that I had previously done.
Here in Gerber-Tobler's company kindergarten I look after
pre-school children during the factory workers' shifts. I teach
them in a playful way, but on account of the numbers have
to be very strict and enforce discipline. Otherwise it wouldn't
work. My relationship to the individual children is less close
than it was in Paris or even Lucerne. I think with gratitude
of how I have always been lucky in my jobs so far. Patron
Gerber is very interested in the kindergarten; he often drops
in and asks whether I need something or if everything is going
as per my satisfaction.

Here in Bern I am free after my intense working days as well
as on Saturday afternoons and all day Sunday, which gives me
time to explore the city and its surroundings.

I consider myself lucky to now be able to get to know
Bern, our capital city, after St. Gallen, Cham, Zug, Paris and
Lucerne. All the cities in which I have so far lived have something special about them and are beautiful in their own way.
Here I enjoy long walks along the Aare, the pretty, historic
Old Town with the Zytglogge Tower, which is famous for
its astronomic clock and glockenspiel, as well as the iconic
sandstone buildings with their countless arcades that charac-
terize the city. Occasionally I pay a visit to the bears in the
well known Bear Pit or Dählhölzli Zoo.

On the way home today I treat myself to a hazelnut lebkuchen from Reinhold, which is traditionally decorated with a bear.

While I enjoy the first bite, I think of how many other enchanting places there are to discover in the world. And I am determined to see as many of them as possible with my own eyes. Bern will not be my last stop.

Wednesday, 11 November 1942

German and Italian troops occupy Vichy France. Switzerland is thus completely surrounded by the Axis powers. The Swiss National Council tells its people that in case of war, Switzerland will defend itself to the last.

1943

Bern ~ Thursday, 7 January 1943

Every year after Christmas when I see the countless, no longer decorated Christmas trees by the side of the road, I think of Madeleine. On one of our walks after my first Christmas in Paris, she asked me indignantly why people took their Christmas trees, which they had decorated with such care, and left them so carelessly out in the cold. She found it terribly sad. And so I told her a story, in the hopes that it would cheer her up:

After Christmas, usually on 6 January, the day on which, according to the Bible, the Three Kings reached the stable in Bethlehem, most people take the decorations off their Christmas trees. The Camus family do so as well. Oskar, their Christmas tree, has done his duty. They carefully pack away shining baubles, glittering ornaments and delicate lace in tissue paper-lined boxes and store them in the attic. Then, with a great effort, Father carries the bulky tree out of the living room. Oskar, the tree, is outraged by this action and angrily drops as many needles as possible in defiance of his fate. It's no use. Oskar, who was so recently a Christmas tree shining in his magnificence, ends up as a desolate, naked thing on the side of the road in the icy winter cold. Oskar is freezing and lonely. Shivering, he looks around, wishing he had a hat and scarf. In this distance he can make out fellow sufferers, but they are standing too far away and don't hear his cries. The next day, while it is still dark, a huge lorry drives up. Oskar, still half asleep, flies in a high arc onto the truck bed and lands roughly. Again he loses countless needles, which are no longer totally green. The lorry shudders and drives off, stopping again a few moments later. With a dull thud a second former Christmas tree lands directly on top of Oskar. Full of joy, the two begin to exchange their stories.

Hugo was, generally speaking, pretty lucky – he was decorated with beautiful gold baubles and wondered at by many pairs of eyes. On Christmas Eve his branches were even hung with a few star-spraying sparklers, which brought him increased admiration, especially from the children. Unexpectedly, he met the same sudden fate as Oskar.

While the two of them are talking, they hardly notice that more and more discarded trees are joining them. When they reach the edge of the city, the trees are unloaded. There are so many of them – a whole Christmas tree cemetery! Oskar can hardly believe his luck. Boredom is over – there are so many friends for him here! The Christmas trees celebrate rowdily, their cheerful chatter echoing through the stillness all night long. Not a single one wishes that he were back in a living room or to be hung again with heavy decorations!

Boncourt ~
Saturday, 2 October 1943

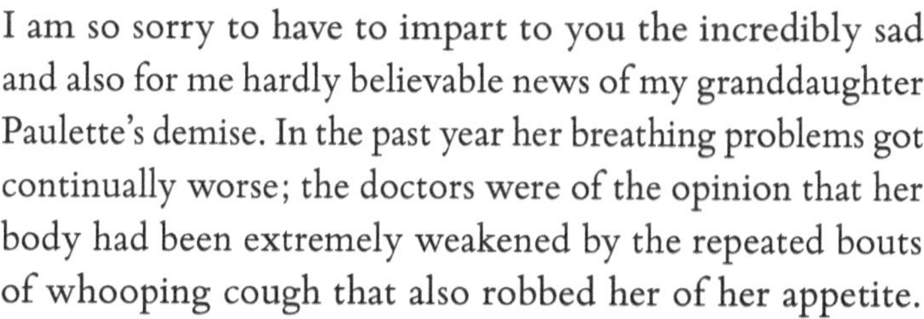

My dear Claire,

I am so sorry to have to impart to you the incredibly sad and also for me hardly believable news of my granddaughter Paulette's demise. In the past year her breathing problems got continually worse; the doctors were of the opinion that her body had been extremely weakened by the repeated bouts of whooping cough that also robbed her of her appetite.

Repeated cures in Normandy unfortunately failed to have the desired effect and when Paulette grew ill with a lung infection, in addition to whooping cough, even the best doctor couldn't help her. We are all shocked and deeply saddened that our beautiful, gentle girl was only allowed eleven years of life. The Countess, her husband and the children are all suffering from shock. Especially the little ones can't understand that their big sister won't be coming back.

Due to the current situation, Madame Deschamps and I weren't even allowed to attend the funeral of our granddaughter three days ago. At this distance we are hardly able to support our daughter and her remaining five children, the youngest of whom – Cloë – you don't yet know.

I know how much you love the children and therefore it was an urgent need for me to tell you of Paulette's death. Please pray for her soul as well as the rest of the family.

I hope that things are better for you and send you, my dear Claire, my best greetings and wishes.

Henry Deschamps

Bern ~ Thursday, 21 October 1943

Since learning of Paulette's death I have been utterly cast down. Hardly a waking hour goes by in which I don't think of the sweet little girl who is no longer with us. I find it unbelievable and, although I know that Paulette is dead, it hasn't really hit me yet.

If I could have a free wish on my birthday today, I would wish the little girl back. I can't imagine how awful it must have been for Monsieur and Madame to have to bury their own child. One would probably give one's own life in order to keep one's child alive. Suddenly I am struck by thoughts of how many parents every day have had to bury their children since this awful war began in Europe. Some of them in undignified circumstances. And many soldiers die far away from home. Will they ever come to rest in their homeland?

These are dark thoughts that cloud my mood on my birthday. Even though I am determined that every birthday I will look back with gratitude on the previous year and treat myself to something special, I am not in the mood for that today. In keeping with my feelings, the weather is grey, wet and bleak. In the afternoon, thick trails of fog were already creeping through the streets like a ghost. I pass the Holy Trinity Church and decide to spend this year's birthday in silence, to pray and to light a candle for Paulette.

Bern ~ Monday, 22 November 1943

It is just before four o'clock in the morning when Lydia and I creep out of my tiny staff bedroom. Patches of fog hang in the streets and we are grateful for our winter coats. I have draped my shoulders in a thick woollen shawl from my days in Paris; my leather-gloved hands grip the handle of my favourite handbag. We march briskly towards the city centre, in suspense about what the day will bring. For both of us it is our first time visiting the traditional Onion Market, an institution in Bern. The Gerber family is expecting visitors, with whom they wish to visit the market. My boss has kindly given me — and the rest of the staff — a day off. By coincidence, Lydia's kindergarten is closed for renovation for three days, so she was able to use the opportunity to visit me.

Mr Gerber, my boss and, in his words, an original Bernese, reckons that the setting up of the market stalls, when the painstakingly plaited strings of onion and garlic are brought into the city by the farmers and artistically arranged, is a unique experience that I shouldn't miss. We are thus already out and about at such an early hour, and don't seem to be the only ones. The closer we come to the upper Old Town, the more figures hurry ghost-like through the narrow streets with the same destination as us. I link my arm through Lydia's and, as we pass over the Kornhaus Bridge, shiver from the cold and from pleasant butterflies of anticipation. At the square with the same name as the bridge, we watch as potential customers bargain with market traders. It seems as though some of the most keen got up extra early in order to be sure of getting the most beautiful creations, because already the first sales are being made. We wonder whether at six o'clock, when the market officially opens, it will already have the atmosphere of an end-of-day sale. Mr Gerber had said that fifty tonnes of goods are up for sale on this day. Fifty tonnes ought to be enough, although I can't really imagine what that amount looks like.

We watch in fascination as the farmers' wives lay out their handmade onion and garlic plaits on their market stalls. To our astonishment, they also conjure up artistically plaited wreaths and other shapes. The most beautiful creations are hung at the side of the display, probably to attract as many customers as possible.

To shake off the cold that is slowly creeping into our bodies from the wet ground, despite our thick clothing, we march on. Coffee is being sold at one stall and so we treat ourselves to a standing breakfast of warming coffee and a croissant.

Fog hangs softly over the capital city, but that doesn't stop us from strolling across National Square and through the neighbouring streets. The majority of the goods on offer consists of onions and garlic in all possible forms, but one can also find other winter vegetables, pip fruit, nuts and pastries as well as occasional ceramics. On this special day, restaurants serve cheesy onions, onion cake, onion sausage or onion soup, which spread a spicy smell through the air.

At lunch, Lydia asks me if I still miss France so much. The question is unexpected. Although I don't think about it all the time, I have to admit that I miss the children a lot. Since then, work has never been the same. I try to suppress the matter and am no longer sure if France still holds such appeal for me now that I know it is inaccessible. What if I knew I could go back tomorrow? Would I be as on fire to go back as I imagine?

After we have closely inspected what is on offer at the market, it seems time to buy something as well. After much consideration I decide on an onion wreath decorated with flowers and a traditional garlic plait, which I would like to take to my mother in St. Gallen at the next opportunity. I am sure she has never seen anything like it. Lydia buys a lot and I have to laugh when I imagine her taking everything back to Zug by train. We walk through the arcaded shopping passages and past the old sandstone buildings to the station, from where Lydia will be travelling home. Before we say our goodbyes, we drink a hot *Glühwein* and snack on the *Magenbrot* that we had bought earlier. Confetti suddenly flies at us from out of nowhere. We look confused and two locals explain to us that the young and still-young celebrate the end of the Onion Market with a confetti fight. The streets turn into a sea of colour – what a beautiful, happy moment in these bleak times, I think.

1944

Bern ~ Sunday, 27 February 1944

Exhausted, I sink into the only chair in my room. It is made of wood and is hard and uncomfortable. I look at my image in the mirror, which I hung over the little table myself, in order to make a French-style dressing table. I am wearing my favourite pink blouse, combined with a pencil skirt from Paris that is extravagant for Bern. This was probably too provocative, I think with consternation. What a thought-provoking evening. A few hours ago I had been looking forward to the impending dinner with my boss. He had already invited me for a meal several times to discuss the company kindergarten with me. We had always conversed animatedly, never lacking for topics or limiting ourselves only to business. I did wonder why he had invited me for dinner on a Sunday evening this time, but thought that it was probably just that he is a busy businessman who has plenty of appointments during the week. The evening was different than usual. More charming, with candlelight, wine and, at the end, a present of a box of my favourite truffles from the Loeb department store. I don't know how he knew that I especially like them. Mr Gerber, who was very smartly dressed, insisted that we walk home after dinner – after all, we had eaten well and a digestive walk wouldn't hurt. His hand repeatedly brushed against mine, at first apparently by accident, but then more obviously. I didn't know how to react and wondered whether he was aware of his attractiveness. I would be lying if I said that I hadn't enjoyed the evening. The tingling was exciting. But to enter into a liaison with the boss is not a good idea. It would be unheard of. Where would it lead?

Geneva ~
Monday, 20 March 1944

Dear Claire,

I don't know if you still remember our encounter in the South
of France. For my part, I have not forgotten and have often
wondered how you are.

Since the Swiss Union for War-Damaged Children was inte-
grated into the Swiss Red Cross on the order of the National
Council in 1942, I have been back in Switzerland and stationed
at the headquarters of the Red Cross in Geneva, where I organize and coordinate convalescence for war-disabled children.
The aim is to improve the children's poor health and to allow
them a couple of carefree weeks, whether with a host family
or in one of our holiday residences. If the children are strong
enough we make outings with them, play, sing and do crafts.

This year, our aim is to take in 40,000 children from countries
at war for three months each. We are looking for carers from
different professional backgrounds, such as nurses, kindergarten teachers, doctors and cooks, who will support our
undertaking during deployments of several weeks or months.

I decided to look for you, as I can imagine that you would be
a good candidate for such a deployment and had the impression
when we met that you are genuinely interested in our work.

I got your address through the Society of Swiss Repatriates,
but have no idea what you are currently doing, if you would

be available and if you would be interested in working for the Swiss Red Cross.

The Swiss Red Cross covers food and board as well as travel costs during a deployment. A small amount of pocket money – 20 francs – is also paid every month.

Please let me know if you are available and if I can count on your valuable support. The solidarity of our volunteers is unique and a good experience. I am looking forward to hearing from you, no matter whether you want to accept or decline my offer.

Best wishes from the heart of West Switzerland!

Yours,
Käthi Oberholzer

Bern ~
Saturday, 15 April 1944

Dear Mr Deschamps,

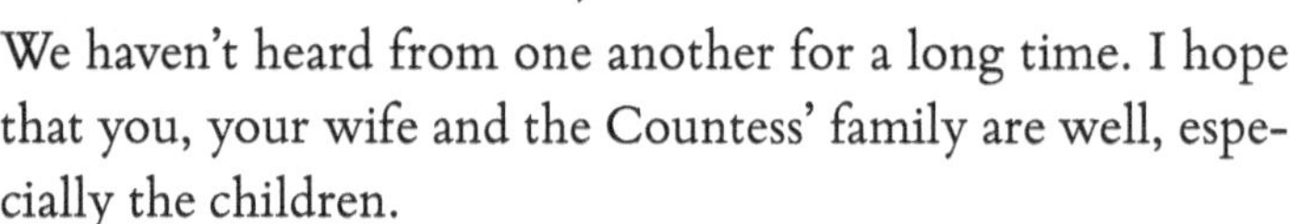

We haven't heard from one another for a long time. I hope that you, your wife and the Countess' family are well, especially the children.

After having spent nearly two years in Bern, which I have largely enjoyed, my employment here is ending on 23 April. I already have my next job lined up. After two weeks of holiday in St. Gallen I will be travelling to Alpnach, to work in childcare for the Swiss Red Cross. Children from war-torn areas, who have become ill, malnourished, traumatized or injured due to the effects of war, are given the opportunity to recover physically and psychologically during a three- to six-month stay. It is a matter of great personal importance to be able to help the weakest victims of this awful war; the Red Cross' initiative seems to me to be a valuable and purposeful one and I am looking forward to a new challenge.

With this short letter I wanted to inform you of my new address and send you my best wishes.

Claire Widmer

St. Gallen ~ Saturday, 22 April 1944

'**D**amn it!' Shocked and surprised, I look up from my work. It is the first time in my life that I have heard my mother swear. We are crouching over the bathtub in my parents' house.

Yesterday, an enormous amount of Argentinian honey from the tropical rainforest of Gran Chaco Sudamericano was delivered to us. Nobody knew in advance about the delivery from overseas and we had difficulty finding space in the house and cellar for all the tubs. Still, Eugen had enclosed a letter in which he gave us detailed instructions on what to do with the honey. The big barrels must be heated so that the honey will become runny. Then it should be poured into 250g or 500g jars and labelled. Finally, this delicacy should be sold in Arthur's bakery and at the market for three or five francs a jar.

It is doubtful that my brother has ever filled honey jars himself. After being warmed in the bathtub, the sticky mass clings intractably to the spoons and plastic tubs and can hardly be poured into the waiting screw-top jars. It looks as though we are going to be busy for some time.

Alpnach ~ Saturday, 10 May 1944

Time and again I am amazed by what life or fate has in store. Whenever I think that I am without a job, a door opens unexpectedly. Whatever ones believes in or chooses to call these acts of providence, it is bewildering and has brought me to my current position in Alpnach, at the foot of the Pilatus in Central Switzerland.

In the Swiss Red Cross' holiday residence I am responsible for a group of eight children. The mountain idyll is a stark contrast to the circumstances from which the children have come to us. They are not used to surroundings free of rubble and ruins. Even though some of them suffer from homesickness, all of them start blooming after a short period of time. Their thin legs grow stronger and can better carry them across the lush meadows.

George, a sweet, ten-year-old boy from Portsmouth in the South of England, has grown especially dear to me. Even though he is very reserved and shy, he is opening up to me. He has jaunty freckles on his cheeks, sits in my lap in his brown shorts and red, knee-high socks and tells me about his arduous journey from home. He travelled by boat from the English coastal city to Le Havre in France, then by train to the Swiss border.

At the border station of Basel, where they arrived in the morning, all the children were given two bowls of sausage soup in the station restaurant – his first warm meal in months, so George tells me. After they had eaten, the children were cleaned and disinfected in the bathing complex by the Swiss Border Sanitation Service. The little English boy was amused by the sight of so many carers in dark bathing suits and giggled as he told me about it. The children were thoroughly scrubbed from top to bottom. Then they were given fresh clothing. Their suitcases, including the spartan contents, were also disinfected.

As I am aware, everything possible is done to avoid the project being endangered by accidentally introduced diseases. The children are finally given a thorough examination by border control doctors and, if necessary, sent to Schaffhausen Quarantine Camp for a week. Even the children who are cleared of primary diseases and have arrived here in Alpnach are very weak. We make them stronger with good food and bed rest. The children with war wounds, some of them even amputees, are cared for by nurses. When the weather is fine they push the beds onto the balcony in the afternoon, so that the children can get some sun, as walking or playing outside isn't possible for these poor creatures. How awful, I think, as my gaze wanders over the playground on which my charges are larking about. George's red-blond hair tickling my face, I enjoy the beautiful view from up here over Lake Alpnach. Only now do I notice that this sweet little rascal has the English version of my half-brother Georg's name – maybe that's why I feel such a connection.

Alpnach ~ Friday, 23 June 1944

This afternoon I am taking a short walk with the oldest
children in my group. Behind the stately home in which
we are living, there is a path through a lush, green meadow.
We follow the path, passing through an area of woodland,
and after a short march come to a clearing that is astonish-
ingly flat after the steep approach and from where, in good
weather such as today's, one can even see a few inlets of Lake
Lucerne. The boys in the group are especially fast and I have
to really rush to keep up with them. It's gratifying to watch
this energy when I think that a few weeks ago these same
boys could barely stand on their own two feet, so weak were
they when they arrived. I tell the children to sit down. Each
of them has a drawing pad and pencils with them. I task
the wild little things with drawing a subject of their liking
with the materials we have brought with us. The best will
be rewarded with an extra treat at breaktime. I set the task
in English and French, which are the languages spoken by the
children in my group.

Then I sit down in the grass, although not before I have spread
out a small woollen blanket so as not to ruin my nice skirt.

The children set to work, well-behaved, concentrated and deep in thought. After a quarter of an hour I stand up, straighten the thin belt at my waist, smooth my spotted jacket and go to inspect their work.

George is drawing tree top after tree top – slowly, a forest emerges on his piece of paper. Adeline sketches an alpine swift that moves in circles above us, trilling loudly. François is drawing in great detail the hiking rucksack that lies in the grass in front of him. He seems to be the most talented of all when it comes to drawing.

At breaktime, each child gets an apple and a piece of bread and I give François his prize, a *Schoggistengeli*. I am moved when I see that he has broken it into five equal pieces and is sharing it out amongst the children.

Alpnach ~ Sunday, 16 July 1944

Dear Lydia,

As always, I hope that my letter finds you in the best of health.

After the time I have spent in the cities of Paris, Lucerne and Bern, I am delighting in the mountain idyll of Alpnach, where I am currently very much enjoying working as a kindergarten teacher in the Swiss Red Cross' holiday residence.

For a long time after I returned from France I couldn't imagine ever finding a job that would fulfil me in the same way again. But here I am happy and balanced. My work is meaningful and my colleagues interesting to talk to. The solidarity between the volunteers and the friendships that spring up are also unique. Maybe because all of us have taken on Henry Dunant's principles and have come to serve those that need it most.

The enquiry as to whether I would be interested in working for the Swiss Red Cross came at the perfect time for me. I was becoming increasingly uncertain in Bern, which wasn't really to do with my work but rather with the fact that I felt cornered by Mr Gerber. As I told you before, he is an excellent boss. He is also a widower with three young children. He invited me more and more often to dinner, in order to talk about the kindergarten. I felt it my duty to accept the invitations and at first I enjoyed his compliments, which were initially to do with my work but then became more personal. We always had a lot to talk about. More invitations for walks followed, during which he more or less subtly tried to take my hand and suggested that we address one another informally. I was given flowers and chocolates as presents. Anxiety overcame me and I was annoyed by my naivety. It dawned on me that he saw me as a potential partner, perhaps even a replacement mother for his children. Who could blame him? Several times he poured his heart out to me, telling me how hard it was to find a suitable nanny who could meet his high standards. He would always compare them with his dead wife. As though escaping, I gave up my position in Bern as soon as I got the job offer from Alpnach. My boss took my decision calmly and we left one another on good terms, which was important to me.

Interestingly, my family seems to be relieved to know that I am in Switzerland, even if we don't see each other more often or have more contact than we did when I was abroad.

When I look out over Lake Lucerne, in the distance I can make out Heiligkreuz Abbey, which is full of fond memories for me. Do you remember how we sometimes used to sneak into one another's curtained beds in the night, where we whispered and giggled? At morning roll call the next day Sister Agnes used to say in a strict voice, 'It was too loud in the blue dormitory – far too loud!' which only made us start giggling again in secret. There were never any sanctions. Now I am the one who makes nightly rounds of the dormitories and insists on quiet – though half-heartedly, because I let the children have this pleasure. After an evening on which it's taken a while for silence to descend, there follows automatically one on which they all voluntarily crawl into bed.

I would really like to make a trip to Heiligkreuz Abbey on one of my free days. It would be nice to take the opportunity to see you – now that the days are so long, an outing is really worth it.

I hope to see you soon and send my love.

Yours,
Claire

Alpnach ~ Friday, 25 August 1944

The radio crackles alarmingly but we can still understand the monotone voice of the announcer. More and more colleagues stream into the staffroom and gather around the little black box. Word of the news had spread quickly. The announcer is saying:

'In recent weeks prices on the black market grew so much that a large number of Parisian citizens couldn't pay for food – the number of the starving increased rapidly. Parisians joined the Résistance in even greater numbers. As did three German officers of the occupation, namely Kurt Hälker, Hans Heisel and Karl-Heinz Gerstner, who informed their new colleagues of planned arrests and Hitler's order to destroy Paris' industry.

'After the rapid Allied advance towards the French capital, the Parisian metro, gendarmerie and police went on strike on 10 August; postmen went on strike on 16 August. The German troops reacted by shooting 35 French youths at 'Carrefour des Cascades' in the Bois de Boulogne on the night of 16 August. As more and more workers joined the strike movement, a general strike was called on 18 August, the day on which all members of the Résistance were called upon to mobilize.

'Today, in contravention of the Führer's express order of 23 August that Paris must not be allowed to fall into enemy hands – or only as a field of rubble – and after initial resistance, the German Infantry General and Supreme Commander of the Greater Paris Wehrmacht, Dietrich von Choltitz, surrendered to the approaching resistance fighters and Allied troops with the 2nd French Tank Division at their head.

'At around 12:20pm the tricolour was raised on the Eiffel Tower and, shortly after, on the Arc de Triomphe. At 2:45pm General von Choltitz handed a nearly undamaged Paris over to Henri Rol-Tanguy, the Parisian leader of the Résistance, and shortly afterwards to the French General Major Leclerc and the American General Bradley. A victory parade of tanks decorated with flags and flowers took place on the Champs-Elysées this evening. An excited crowd lined the streets, women blew kisses, men raised their fists in the air and showed their excitement to the occupiers. Paris is free!'

Cheers erupt in the room, but I remain sitting in silence. I cannot imagine all that has happened in my beloved Paris in the last days, weeks and months. Shootings in the Bois de Boulogne, where I used to go walking with the children, where they larked about, laughed and played on the playground. Starving people, who joined the resistance out of despair and so risked their lives in the hope that their situation would soon improve. What might have happened in my street? Did its inhabitants witness the execution of the youths in the nearby park?

I am tapped cautiously on the shoulder. It is Walter, one of the Red Cross doctors. 'Claire, go to bed and rest.'

I look up furtively. I hadn't noticed that the staffroom had emptied. Although I am too wound up to sleep, I go to my room. My Paris has really been freed!

Boncourt ~
Sunday, 27 August 1944

My dear Claire,

No doubt you have heard of the current developments in France
and, especially, Paris. I can well imagine that you must be very
moved as well. For my part, I am extremely happy and relieved
about the end of the occupation. The Count immediately left
the castle in Ligny in order to clear up the situation in Paris
and to inspect his property. He also learned that the borders
are open again and so I am planning to undertake a journey
to Paris soon, about which I will of course tell you.

In the meantime, dear Claire, my best wishes.
Henry Deschamps

Paris ~
Tuesday, 19 September 1944

My dear Claire,

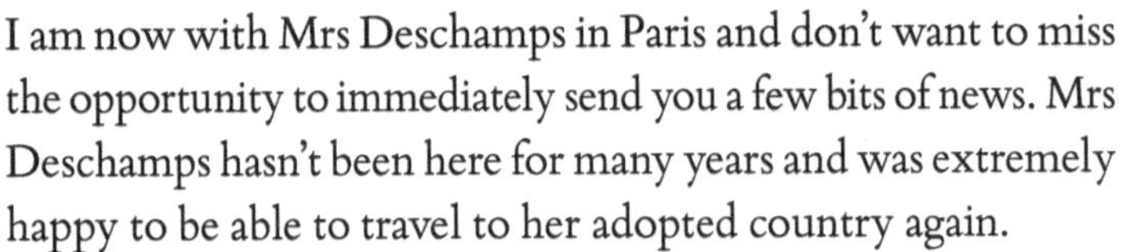

I am now with Mrs Deschamps in Paris and don't want to miss
the opportunity to immediately send you a few bits of news. Mrs
Deschamps hasn't been here for many years and was extremely
happy to be able to travel to her adopted country again.

We found the Countess and children in good form. Thank
God for that! They were all naturally very pleased that they
can move freely once again. They found the apartment in Rue
Eugène Labiche in a good state. It seems as though nobody

had lived there in the meantime and only a few renovations are necessary. How lucky – not everything is so good! On the night of 26 August fifty German Luftwaffe planes dropped bombs on Paris, destroying nearly six hundred buildings and killing over two hundred people. The scars of war are plain to see, but despite that Paris seems to have found its way back to a certain normality – a liberating feeling!

Yesterday evening boisterous youths ran through the streets, happily chorusing, 'The potato bugs are gone! The potato bugs are gone!'

Apparently this was the nickname of the occupiers, due to their love of potatoes and the colour of their uniforms. People dare to go outside in the evening once again. Up until now the danger of lone snipers was still too great, but now most collaborators seem to have been caught. The state's legal clean-up apparatus is showing effects.

We are planning to travel to Bon-Hôtel Castle this coming weekend, where we will visit our granddaughter Paulette's grave for the first time. Even if this is associated with many painful memories, we will also be happy that we are allowed to do it. For a long time, the Countess was uncertain as to whether Paulette's body should be exhumed after the war and brought to the family grave in Paris. Now both the Count and Countess are leaning towards erecting a suitable monument to their daughter in the castle gardens.

As you have told me, you are finding your current position with the Swiss Red Cross very fulfilling, which pleases me greatly. I myself am closely linked to the Swiss Red Cross as a donor and appreciate the enormous amount of work carried out by countless volunteers in service to humanity. Above all, I follow the children's initiatives with great interest.

It is not my intention to put you into a dilemma. Nevertheless, now that the global situation has improved, I would like to once again offer you a position with my daughter. As you can imagine, the Countess asked after you and so we began to converse. In the years since your departure, my daughter hasn't been able to find anyone who could so subtly integrate into family life and who understood how to competently, firmly but lovingly raise the children. It is very rare – of that I can assure you, my dear Claire – and therefore we would gladly have your esteemed services again.

We do not expect an immediate response from you – give yourself time.

And now my best wishes,

Henry Deschamps

Paris ~ Autumn 1944

Although it's a mild autumn afternoon in Paris, I am shivering. I pull my coat closely around me and wish I had my scarf to hand. 1178 days have passed since the last time I was here. On the outside, nothing has changed – everything seems the same. New things are awaiting me, however: Paulette is no longer there, the three children I know have grown,

I have only seen Antoine once and I don't know little Cloë
at all. Familiar and yet still unknown, I think. I carefully place
my brown leather suitcase on the pavement and ring the bell
at Number Ten, Rue Eugène Labiche.

1945

Monday, 7 May 1945

After Hitler's suicide in Berlin on 30 April, Germany surrenders unconditionally to the Western forces and, a day later, to the Soviet Union.

Wednesday, 9 May 1945

With the coming into effect of the surrender, the Second World War in Europe ends.

Monday, 20 August 1945

Switzerland dismisses its General, active service ends and the army is demobilized.

Sunday, 2 September 1945

The Japanese Empire surrenders unconditionally after the dropping of the atomic bombs. The Second World War is over.

Epilogue

After her final return to Switzerland in autumn 1947, my grandmother met her future husband, Albert, in Gossau St. Gallen. She became a mother to three children. Until the end of the 1970s my grandparents ran a bakery in Winterthur.

My grandmother kept much from her time in France for her whole life, sometimes to the amusement of my grandfather: the knife rests on the table on Sunday, the finger bowls filled with lukewarm water and a slice of lemon, the Roger Gallet soaps and the melons, which back then were still unknown and a real delicacy.

On her 80th birthday we travelled to Paris together and visited the places in the French capital that she could remember, including Rue Eugène Labiche and the Bois de Boulogne park.

My grandmother died in June 2010 in Winterthur. She was 91 years old. I had felt very close to her while she was alive, but my admiration for her has only grown during the research for this book. Thank you for everything, Grosi!

My deepest thanks go to

my grandmother	for inspiring me to live life to the fullest
my parents	without you, I wouldn't be who I am today
Renzil	for your unconditional love
Henry and Viola	through you, I have been able to experience a new form of love
Markus and Monica	life is more fun with you in it.

Glossary

Canton	Switzerland is divided into 26 member states, known as cantons
Embroiderer's home	from a certain time, many embroiderers kept embroidery machines at home and took on commissions. They were not employed by anyone, but obtained commissions and materials via textile trade middlemen and carried out the work at home.
Escargot aux	round/spiral-shaped raisin pastry raisins
Friandise	sweet
Führer	title occupied by Adolf Hitler (translates as 'leader')
Glühwein	mulled wine
Lebkuchen	a spiced, soft biscuit
Luftwaffe	German Air Force
Madame	Mrs
Mademoiselle	Miss

Magenbrot	thin, sometimes glazed *lebkuchen*
Mailänderli	Swiss Christmas biscuits: butter biscuits with a light lemon flavour
Monsieur	Mr
Rappen	Swiss centimes
Rösti	a fried potato patty
Pip fruit	apples and pears collectively
Savoir-vivre	ability to live life well, with enjoyment and good manners
Schoggistengeli	chocolate bar
Tartelette aux framboises	raspberry tart
Wehrmacht	German military (during the Nazi period)

Klara & Claire: Important Sites in France

Klara & Claire: Important Sites in Switzerland

Memories of my Grandmother

www.ingramcontent.com/pod-product-compliance
Lightning Source LLC
LaVergne TN
LVHW051525170726
843492LV00006B/1628